PRAISE FOR RICK BASS
AND *The Diezmo*

"Rick Bass is one of our best writers. *The Diezmo* is further proof; a vivid, graphic, harrowing tale of wild men and bad blood, a fable universal and timeless in its application."
— KENT HARUF

"Bass is without peer when he writes about characters in their landscape." — *Denver Post*

"Mesmerizing."
— *Arizona Daily Star,* Top Ten Southwest Books of the Year

"The best literary adventure story I've read since *Legends of the Fall.*" — HOWARD FRANK MOSHER

"[*The Diezmo*] achieves the molten beauty, compassion, and longing for justice found in Stephen Crane's *Red Badge of Courage* and the novels of B. Traven and Cormac McCarthy."
— *Booklist,* starred review

"Recaptures the bravado of many of those who joined the expedition ... a compellingly effective blend of [history and fiction]." — *Washington Post Book World*

"A potent story." — *Chicago Tribune*

"A masterpiece." — *Playboy*

"No other living American writer can drop us into the wild, wild West or a Texas countryside like Rick Bass. Writing with empathy and great humility, he makes characters we can touch."
— *The Rake*

The
Diezmo

Rick Bass

A MARINER BOOK
HOUGHTON MIFFLIN COMPANY
BOSTON · NEW YORK

First Mariner Books edition 2006

For information about permission to reproduce selections from
this book, write to Permissions, Houghton Mifflin Company,
215 Park Avenue South, New York, New York 10003.

Visit our Web site: www.houghtonmifflinbooks.com.

Library of Congress Cataloging-in-Publication Data

Bass, Rick, date.
The Diezmo / Rick Bass.
p.   cm.
ISBN 0-395-92617-3
1. Texan Mier Expedition (1842–1844) — Fiction. 2. Mexican-
American Border Region — Fiction. 3. Texas — History — To
1846 — Fiction. 4. Americans — Mexico — Fiction. 5. Prisoners
of war — Fiction., 6. Torture victims — Fiction.   I. Title.
PS3552.A8213D54 2005
813'.54 — dc22   2004062755

ISBN-13: 978-0-618-71050-8 (pbk.)
ISBN-10: 0-618-71050-7 (pbk.)

Printed in the United States of America

Book design by Robert Overholtzer

MP 10 9 8 7 6 5 4 3 2 1

For Elizabeth, Mary Katherine, Lowry

The Diezmo

1

SUMMONS

I WAS AS WILD for glory as any of us. Before too much time had passed, we had all changed our minds, had given up on dreams of glory and were fighting only to win. And not too much longer after that, all that was on our minds was a good cool drink of water; and before it was over, all any of us wanted was simply to get back home.

How much of it was hate, and how much love? In our expedition, there was plenty of both. Our commanders, Thomas Jefferson Green (named for his great-uncle in Virginia) and Captain William S. Fisher, were adept from the start at braiding the two together, love and hate, in such a fashion as ultimately to possess us. We became a rope that they kept coiled, and then used for their purposes — Thomas Jefferson Green pursuing love, I think, while Fisher was intent on chasing down his hatred. It's a miracle that any of us got out alive, and though I was only sixteen when they came riding through, asking for volunteers, I do not hold them accountable for my own free-will choice. They were just passing through: one counseling patriotism, the other vengeance. Between them, they caught the few of us who were left unclaimed by that one emotion or the other.

The purpose of our militia, Fisher informed us, would be to hunt down a band of infidels, Mexican nationals, who had come across the new border of Texas and staged an attack on San Antonio. There would be plenty of fighting, he assured us, all we could ever wish for. The glory existed just beyond our reach, he told us, but only barely. All we had to do was go out and search for it, he promised, and it would be delivered to us.

Too young to have fought at the Alamo, my friend James Shepherd and I thought we had missed our opportunity for war. We thought that with the victory at San Jacinto less than a month after the fall of the Alamo, a disgusting wave of peace and softness had settled on the land and that weakness had come flooding in. We thought our manhood would never be tested.

Thomas Jefferson Green, like his namesake, was in love with his new homeland and the potential of the new republic — he had political aspirations and was said to be one war away from being eminently electable — as popular one day, perhaps, as General Houston himself — while Fisher simply wanted to injure, maim, and destroy.

My own town of LaGrange had a firsthand acquaintance with such sentiments. One of our native sons, Captain Nicholas Dawson, had rushed to the defense of San Antonio against one of General Woll's invasions. It was infuriating to all Texans that Mexico was coming back for more: six years earlier Mexico had surrendered half her nation — the whole of Texas — following Santa Anna's expensive victory at the Alamo and humiliating defeat at San Jacinto — and then the Mexican army, having pinned Dawson into a position of surrender, went ahead and massacred thirty-five of his men, despite the truce. Only five had escaped the terms of the "surrender," including our own Dawson, who spoke ceaselessly of revenge, and how he would never trust the flag of Mexico again.

I had one day helped him repair a fence, through which some of his father's cows had escaped — he was a quiet, strong, pleasant young man, only four years older than I was — though when he came back from the Dawson Expedition his arm was shattered and held by a makeshift sling, a saber scar ran across his thigh, and he was no longer pleasant but always angry and frightened.

So we knew, or should have known, what we were getting into, but we couldn't help it.

A great victory had been achieved at San Jacinto, and there was no call, save pride and fury, to risk ourselves now. We should have let the bandits be. We should never have joined when Captain Fisher and Captain Green came calling. And having joined their militia, we should have pulled up shy at the Rio Grande, letting Mexico understand that we would defend our newly gained territory, but we should never have gone on into their country.

Five hundred of us left LaGrange that day — three hundred and eight of us would go on to cross the river into Mexico, and only a handful returned. That was fifty years ago, and whenever young people ask, I tell them that there is no shortage of war in the world, and that wars always come looking for someone to fight them — particularly if you're from Texas, with war born in blood. But young people don't often ask and instead plunge into war.

I live on the outskirts of a small town, and I watch mothers, fathers, sisters, and brothers grieve. And it's not only the blood of the enemy and of their own that they grieve, but also the heart's blood — the heart's drying out.

What fun, what glory, what joy must war hold, to summon them thus?

I remember how it seemed that the voice of a beautiful woman was calling and that a spacious country filled with bounty lay just ahead.

Why was I one of the tiny handful who survived the entire journey? I can find no clue, no scrap of order or design, even as I knew all along — or almost all along — that I *would* survive.

Have I subsequently lived in such a fashion as to justify being spared? Have I done anything magnificent, achieved more than those who died would have? Fifty years later — a farmer of stock, a raiser of goats, sheep, and cattle, a grower of corn and cotton — I can find no reason for my survival, but then I can find no good reason for having crossed the border in the first place.

The night before Green and Fisher arrived, I had been troubled by dreams. In the first dream, my friend James Shepherd and I were camped along the James River, which was where we liked to go in the summer to fish for catfish. We could catch them closer to home, in the lower meandering of the muddy Brazos; but in the James River, farther up into the hills, the water ran clearer and faster and the fish tasted better. It was Comanche country, though, and we usually went there only in the early summer, when the People, as the Comanches called themselves, had gone north to hunt buffalo.

There was nothing Shepherd and I loved more in the world than to eat catfish from the James. There was no finer food, no finer times than on those days and nights when we camped beside the clear-running river and feasted on catfish and dreamed about the shape our lives might take. James Shepherd was going to be governor of Texas, or a senator at least, while I, James Alexander, was less sure of my role. I was the better student, and I thought for a while that I might become a physician. (Shepherd, on the other hand, was troubled by the sight of blood, so much so that I had to clean and prepare the fish for him at our meals each morning and evening.)

In this dream that came to me the night before Captains Green and Fisher arrived, Shepherd and I had built a little hut woven from oak and juniper branches — a mound that we latticed and stitched tight with leaves and smaller branches until it resembled the larval encasement of a caddis fly. Such structures kept us warm and dry during even the most violent thunderstorms, and we had spent countless nights in these little huts, bathed in the sweet scent of our oak cook fire, as well as the odor of the crushed juniper bushes and their gin-scented berries.

But in this dream, our earth and branch huts were blazing, and it was neither campfire nor lightning bolt that had ignited them but some dark bird flying through the night, dropping clumps of soil onto every hut. Seconds later, each hut would burst into bright flame, lighting the night.

5

Every hut of our childhood was there, every sanctuary, and the dark bird dropped load after load of rich soil onto our thatched shelters, each one blossoming into flame; and in the dream, we were sometimes in those huts, and other times we were running from the giant bird and the burning huts.

The bird, or whatever it was, seemed to have no knowledge of us personally but was mindlessly intent on destruction, and this cold-blooded indifference made its terror slightly less frightening.

I woke drenched in sweat. The dream was so real I went outside to see if any fires were burning, but the horses were quiet in the barn and there were only a few fireflies circling in the meadow and an owl murmuring down by the creek.

I sat down and wrapped my arms around my legs and watched the stars for a long time, as if waiting for something.

My heart was racing, but the world seemed large and quiet, unperturbed. I went back to bed, and almost immediately upon falling asleep I dreamed the second dream, which was more real than the first.

I was up in the loft of an unfamiliar house. Giant beams were crashing down, breaking through the roof and cracking open the walls, and though the timbers seemed directed toward me, I did not seem to be at risk. This time when I woke, I could not go back to sleep but went outside and sat until dawn, watching and waiting.

I think I knew then that I would survive many tests — that some are chosen for no reason — and the loneliness of that revelation was fierce and complete, involving my greatest fear of being left alone, or behind. It was a fear that had a place in the world. It seemed that I might be called on to keep a certain terror burning in my heart, until finally it burned no more.

Both Green and Fisher rode bay mares, exquisite animals gotten from the spoils of war. Green, a small, chesty man, seeming as wide as he was tall, rode the larger of the two horses, one that was two hands too big for him, so that although he rode it well, he never quite seemed graceful but appeared to expend considerable effort to control the horse. Fisher was taller, more military-looking, and rode a more average-size horse. When the two men were asaddle next to each other, the eye was drawn to Green, as his tall, stiff-legged horse turned and backstepped, cantering and crabbing sideways and rattling her bit. Fisher sat motionless beside such prancings, his eyes searching the crowd, until his gaze narrowed on someone as if that person had disappointed or betrayed him. Then he gazed upon that person with an almost tender forgiveness, but with a fierce, angry curiosity as well, as if asking, *How could you?* As if calling into question all the choices a person had made in a lifetime.

Such was the look that fell upon me that morning they rode into town.

Fisher seemed to study me for hours, but it could only have been seconds. When he finally released me, I turned to search for James Shepherd and saw that he was watching the curious exhibition of Thomas Jefferson Green atop the massive bay, which was turning in tight circles like a copper-colored dervish.

Shepherd saw me and then raised his hand to enlist. He took a step toward the soldiers, who looked so clean and sharp and precise — so *alive* — and I found myself raising my own hand.

We didn't know then that the soldiers, or irregulars, had stopped the day before and bathed in the river and scrubbed their hair and washed their uniforms; they had hung them out to dry in the late-autumn sun, and had brushed and curried their mounts and filed their hoofs in preparation for the next morning's recruiting. We didn't know that they needed only forty more volunteers to attain their desired goal of five hundred, which was what they had ascertained was the ideal strike force, able to travel fast and far and light, yet also sufficient, when under focused discipline, to present formidable, lethal force against the enemy.

Neither did we know that the night before at their encampment the two captains had debated — not quite arguing — about whether to go searching for those final forty in LaGrange, or to veer northwest to Bastrop.

"We only need forty," Fisher had said. "Surely we can find forty in LaGrange."

"But Bastrop is larger," Green said. "And if we *don't* get forty, then we have to go on up to Bastrop anyway, losing two extra days."

They debated some more, out of earshot of their men, and finally decided by Fisher's choosing one of two twigs from Green's fist. The short twig meant they would take the near path to LaGrange, while the longer twig meant traveling directly to Bastrop, bypassing LaGrange. The men, women, and children — the farmers and teachers, mothers and fa-

8

thers, brothers and sisters — slept peacefully in Bastrop, never knowing, never being asked to die, spared, as I would be — but without the choice and the challenge.

In LaGrange, Fisher and Green secured forty-two volunteers. They came from a mix of society: the unschooled and the well educated, the poor and the elite, the sons of ne'er-do-wells, of politicians, of farmers, clerks, and grocers. What burned brightest in us all was a love of the land, with its wild pecan groves and deer and turkey, and the fertile river bottom and endless timber and grasslands.

Surely we would not have had so many wars, had our land not been so beloved — fighting the Indians to the west, and Mexico to the south, as the flow of Appalachian emigrants continued to filter down from out of the highlands.

What our town was like then was the calm in the eye of a storm. We lived in bucolic idyll, and knew it; each morning, dawn's rising found us already out in the fields, working. And paradoxically, it was the pastoral existence, this peace within the whirlwind, that compelled many of us to leave the calm and venture out into the storm. Looking back, I can see clearly the irony and wrong-headedness of it, but back then it seemed to make perfect sense: almost as if such decisions and such notions had been foreordained.

My own family were farmers, Gores and Lowrys from Tennessee, whose ancestors had come down from Wales, pausing for a generation in County Cork before traveling across the Atlantic. Like the other forty-one new recruits, I told my parents goodbye and said that our commanders promised we would be back in two weeks, or three at the most.

We gathered our weapons — a rifle or a pistol, or both — and ammunition, with which we were never wasteful, and packed a lunch, and rode out that afternoon.

Not all of us were young. The eldest was Claudius Toops, a blacksmith of sixty, who enlisted with his son Buster, who was forty, and Buster's own son Andrew, who was twenty. But regardless of rank or age or station in life, that first evening, with the mass of us camped on the banks of the Brazos, we were all in high spirits, conjoined in a new brotherhood.

In the days before our march, the newspapers had been quoting Texas's president, Sam Houston, as saying that regrettably there was no budget for arming militias and bands of patriots such as ours — that "the government will promise nothing but the authority to march, and will furnish such supplies of ammunition as may be needed for the campaign. Volunteers must look to the Valley of the Rio Grande for remuneration," he told reporters, and surely he meant from the other side of the river — the Mexican side. "Our government promises to claim no portion of the spoils," he told the press; "they will be divided among the victors." He finished with one caveat: "The flag of Texas will accompany any such expedition."

And camped there on the Brazos that first night, Captain Green produced with a flourish a tattered paper that he said was our personal marching orders from President Houston himself. The letter was dated October third of that year and addressed not the bandits whom Green and Fisher said we would be chasing, but Mexico's General Woll's surprising attack (with two thousand men) on the southern outpost of San Antonio.

In those early days of the march, our fiddles had not yet been abandoned; a few of the recruits had shoved them into their saddlebags or rode with them tied to their saddles, bouncing and sometimes squealing with a single stray note. And that night, as Green produced and then began to read from his letter, they fell silent, and we listened as intently as if he were President Houston himself.

"Captain Green, my fellow patriot," he read. "You will proceed to the most eligible point on the southwestern frontier of Texas, concentrate with the force now under the command, all troops who may submit to your order, and if you can advance with the prospect of success, into the enemy's territory, you will do so at once. You will receive no troops into your command but such as those who will swear to march across the Rio Grande under your orders, if required by you to do so. If you cross the Rio Grande, you must suffer no surprise, but be always on the alert.

"In battle, let the enemy feel the fierceness of just resentment and retribution. You alone will be held responsible to the government, and sustained by its resources.

"I have the honor to be, Your Obedient Servant, Sam Houston."

Again and again on the campaign, Green would read this letter to us, and he always paused near the end. It was not until much later in the campaign that I found out he had been skipping a sentence.

"You will be controlled by only the most civilized warfare," the sentence read, "and you will find great advantage of exercising great humanity toward the common people."

These words were from a man who had been kicked out of Tennessee for alleged marital scandals, stripped from the

U.S. Senate for alcoholism, and had gone to live with the Indians in east Texas before it was a nation; who had recovered, in that wilderness, and who had gone on to become a chief of the Cherokees, and then the president of a new nation. It was just one sentence, and perhaps a small one — twenty-four words — but in the end, it was all the difference between what was intended and what was done.

We rode south, led by Green and Fisher, the two sometimes glancing at each other but usually staring straight ahead, as if afraid some of us might look back toward home and change our minds. But in the beginning, as we rode south, searching for mysterious bandits, infidels against the republic, we were certain we would win. It was a feeling like the Holy Spirit descending. Your hands and feet tingle. You feel that all is predestined and you have prepared for glory. You cannot imagine loss or the anonymity brought by time.

We secured beef from the ranches and farms we passed. Everything we saw was ours — ours to defend, and then ours to possess. Shepherd and I shared a tent with two boys from Elgin and Navasota. Each night we cleaned our weapons and sharpened our swords. The sound of the steel seemed like the sound of judgment itself, and we were overcome with wonder and relief at having been chosen. We would lead remarkable lives. We had been rescued.

2

GLORY

WE SEETHED WITH the gold light within us, rode across burnished plains gilded in November light, with the dead dry grasses rustling in the north wind. With the Comanches up north hunting buffalo and the Mexicans on the run back behind their border, the country was ours. It was wonderful to see new country, and more wonderful to be in possession of it: to gain ownership of it merely by the act of looking.

Green and Fisher were our captains, but among us were other natural leaders. Bigfoot Wallace, six feet four inches tall and gaunt as a whippet, named for his size-sixteen boots, had been a Texas Ranger — never an officer, because of his uncivilized ways, but a learned soldier nonetheless, in every way the equal of either of our captains and in many ways their superior. He drew a goodly number of men about him at the campfire each night to hear tales of his exploits from past campaigns. He seemed to be a peaceable giant, though it was also said that he had never gone more than a week in his life without engaging in some sort of battle, and it seemed to me, in those first days, that I could see that change beginning to come over him — an abiding and over-arching good humor and generosity becoming slightly more dulled with each passing evening. An anxiety rose in him as day after day passed by without war.

Also prominent within our regiment was the Scotsman Ewen Cameron, who was as dumb as a box of rocks. His strength was so prodigious as to seem supernatural, and like Wallace, he was anxious when in the absence of war. He was less cunning than Wallace, and his anxiety was fed by his fervor. He was a soldier of the Lord, eager to judge and punish, and, in his simplicity, desperate.

And like Bigfoot Wallace, Cameron too had scores of soldiers who gathered around him each evening. And among us was a third group, Lieutenant Somervell's, composed of those who seemed destined to become the politicians and leaders of the republic.

Lieutenant Somervell was another former Texas Ranger — though unlike Wallace, who had been a mere scout, he was a military man through and through. Why Green and Fisher had been assigned leadership, while Somervell, with his precise and military bearing, his caution and dignity, seemed only a participant on the expedition was unclear. I supposed Somervell and others like him could not be kept from war, whether or not their qualities were fully recognized.

We settled into three distinct camps: Fisher's marauders, Green's yeoman nondescripts, and Somervell's dandies. Each man had a chance to tell the others his story if he was fortunate to have one worth telling, though there were many of us who were silent.

For my part, what to tell these rough and angry men: that I was a farmer and a fisherman?

By six short years, the youngest among us had missed the Alamo, and San Jacinto, and the birth of a nation. There was none among us who did not still feel the righteous pride of the victory at San Jacinto, or the pride of the courage and resolve we heard had been displayed at the Alamo during those thirteen days of siege.

John Alexander — no relation to me — had been traveling with Green for weeks, always, it seemed, mere hours behind the enemy. It was Green's fire at which Shepherd and I usually sat, and although John Alexander was too reticent to speak up at the evening storytelling sessions, we learned from him that some days they had been so close to the enemy that coals from their cooking fires had still been glowing and the horse turds in their makeshift corrals still so warm as to be drawing gnats and flies.

He had learned much in the short time he'd spent with Green, he said, but he was growing frustrated, afraid we would never find or catch up to the enemy.

"Those fires," Shepherd asked him, "how did you know they were from the Mexicans?"

John Alexander looked confused as he considered it, and searched for an answer. "Because Captain Green said they were," he said finally.

There were so many others like John Alexander who feared we would never find the enemy, would never engage in combat — that the bandits had already crossed back over the border, and that peace, like a curse, was settling in. But

Fisher, Green, and Somervell told us not to worry, there would be more war.

Sitting around Green's fire, we could hear the singing around Somervell's fire, could see the flame-backed silhouettes of men dancing and cheering. His military men were cut from a different cloth than were we recruits and Fisher's hard cases, but during our journey our differences began to fade, even as our varied desires and motivations began to divide us.

We drifted south, finding occasional traces of the bandits — a whisper in one village, the tale of a pilfered cow in another, the rumor of a stolen ferry, the sound of gunfire, the remains of a large campfire, three days old. I was filled with unease, the sense of having made a poor choice, and I think Shepherd felt it as well. From time to time he looked questioningly over at me.

The sky above us was huge. The tall drying grass of late autumn and early winter rustled before us in waves. The sight of the wind moving across land balanced my unease. I stared forward across the plains and avoided Fisher's and Green's eyes — especially Fisher's. Did they ever look back at their five hundred and consider which ones, or how many, might not return?

We basked in the attentions of the farmers and ranchers. We were given bushels of bread and nuts, chickens and calves, fruits and vegetables. The farther we traveled, the more accustomed we became to such treatment, so that when we did not receive it, there was resentment. Fisher's men, in particular, were quick to take offense, grumbling that they were risking their lives for ungrateful sodbusters and hayseeds, and even some of Somervell's men, despite the lieutenant's obvious displeasure, grew more and more like marauders. It was an astonishment to me how much we required to eat, and the swath we cut, with well over three hundred horses — twelve hundred hooves — cutting our way through the brush, raising sand and dust and eating everything in sight.

Otto Williams was the first man I saw take something without the formality of asking. One day he was near the lead of our ranks as we rode into a small settlement north of Laredo, supposedly looking for the bandits but actually looking for food. It took so much to keep us going that we were less like a military expedition than a very large and extended hunting trip. From the very beginning, I noticed that there were some who were not so much interested in the search for bandits as they were simply in the hunting and the war.

Otto Williams was one of these. As we rode into the little settlement, the townspeople spread to either side of the road and held their possessions close to them: a basket of poor-looking chickens, a sack of flour over each shoulder, a goat on a rope — it was midmorning on a market day — and although they were simply going about their business, the impression it gave, or could have given, I suppose, to a man like Otto Williams, was that these people were coming out to the street to give us these things, that a feast was being prepared in our honor.

And for the first time, without bartering or even asking, Otto Williams simply rode over to a villager who had a young bull tethered to a heavy rope — the bull nearly as large as the old man, whose hair was completely silver — and after drawing his sword from his saddle, Otto Williams brought it down quickly and forcefully. Just as he did so, another rider shifted in front of me, and I thought Otto Williams was only severing the rope that bound the animal, but then I saw that he had struck the animal itself, his razor-sharp sword passing halfway through the animal's neck. The red blade lifted again, bright in the sun, without a sound, and the old man fell back in terror while Williams struck a second and third time before the head — still attached to its halter — fell to the dusty ground, and the animal knelt and fell over.

Williams dismounted and gutted the animal as he would a deer shot on the prairie. He took care not to get his hands or clothing bloody, and when he was done, he gestured to one of his friends to help him lift the carcass onto his horse — as if he intended to eat the whole thing by himself — and then we rode on, silent and tense and changed, with a few more hours of food procured; fuel for the coming war, if only we could find the war.

Some of us were homesick. I myself was troubled by the slightly uneasy feeling that, even though this was a grand and glorious adventure, as well as a just cause, I was leaving behind a land almost as dear to me as life. As we descended into a country of brush and thorns, we missed the soft green hills of home, and as we traveled away from our new country toward one that had been a millennium in the making, we started to see more and more Mexican faces in the villages near the border, and we felt further misgivings.

"When we get home," I told Shepherd one night after dinner, "no matter what time of year it is, I want to go back up to the James and go fishing. I'll let you fish the hole first." I was thinking of the deep water near where we liked to camp and where there were always fish.

James Shepherd looked frightened, but his face shone with a strange intensity — almost a fever.

"Fishing," he snorted. He looked over at the other recruits. "We're going *hunting*. Hunting men," he said.

But none of them paid him any mind, knowing it was only bravado — he was so young — and I knew him better than to take his rebuke seriously. He was only trying to find his place.

Often we spent our time around the campfire writing letters to those we had left behind, exaggerating both our hardships and the heroes' welcomes we received. And not having met the enemy, we speculated about victory. Travis Parvin, a twenty-year-old from Goliad, with his ambition set on the Texas Senate, wrote to his parents that his "unswerving faith in our own fighting abilities, and in the supremacy of the Anglo-Saxon race, has stilled all doubts of our success in this upcoming war." Others spoke of the "miscegenation of the Indian and Hispanic peoples," which had created "a lower breed rendered all the more inferior by a hot, tropical climate which leaves them listless and phlegmatic." Some of the men carried leatherbound journals with elegant fountain pens, and wrote increasingly as the campaign advanced and their boredom grew. Whenever we paused, I'd see one or more of them scribbling away, dipping quill tip cautiously in the inkwell, shielding it and the journal from the blowing grit. The illiterates in our brigade crouched beside the writers, studying the flow of sentences, attempting to discern order and meaning, mystified by the process.

*   *   *

The farther south we got, the more James Shepherd and I talked about death.

In the daytime, Shepherd projected nonchalance, indifference. "If I don't make it back, Jim," he told me, "I want you to have my gun, give my horse to my youngest brother, and tell my family that I died bravely."

In the evenings, he was less confident.

Up on the James River, he had always been exceedingly cautious about the possibility of encountering Comanches. That was understandable, but he had also worried about lesser things — deep-water river crossings, sleeping out at night, and the possibility of getting ill from eating fish that wasn't cooked enough or from dishes that weren't clean. At home, his father had been increasingly critical of his work, so Shepherd was enjoying his first taste of freedom, but an anger was blossoming in him: all his native cautions and fears were finding root in a new, more toxic substrate. We rode on Green's side of the regiment, though Fisher, on the right, searched us out with his yellow eyes.

A half-dozen cliques formed, with cross-pollination occurring daily — subtle betrayals and disappointments, social defections and misunderstandings, intentional disrespect or challenges, and ceaseless miscommunication. Some of us were perceived to be more valuable, more vital to the cause, than others. And we boys from the country were the most expendable, the most unnoticeable of all. Occasionally, even our patriotism was questioned.

"What are your goals?" the interpreter Alfred Thurmond — one of the important ones — asked me and Shepherd one evening, having sensed our weakness, or softness, with our having said hardly a word — an interpreter of silence.

"To do good for my country," I said, with the full earnestness of youth. "To send a message to the enemy, and to make a stand."

Shepherd's answer was more terse, as if he had been pondering and hungering for the question. "Respect," he said. And Alfred Thurmond nodded, as if only that one goal could have a chance of coming true.

James Shepherd watched Captain Fisher with an intensity that bordered on the hypnotic. When Fisher lifted his canteen to drink, Shepherd did the same. When Fisher lifted a hoof of his horse to clean it, Shepherd examined his mount's hooves.

Respect, Shepherd had said. Where might that reside?

I was unobtrusive, almost invisible, in my unremarkableness, my silence and attentiveness. I had a kind of critical awareness of the way that things not said can occupy more space and possess deeper meaning than the things that are spoken. When the cook was distributing the evening beans or that night's stew, I was the one overlooked or not seen, bypassed, not given enough or any at all. I was neither threat nor menace to anyone, possessed neither confidence nor brute strength. Even Green, who had recruited me, could never remember my name. "James Shepherd's friend" was what he and Fisher both called me.

I learned to trust my instincts and imagination, and I detected an unbraiding of currents between Green and Fisher, as well as confusion and drift among Somervell's dandies. Even so, I was unprepared for what happened in Laredo.

We were on our side of the line, among Texans if not yet

Americans: we were still our own separate nation. We had not yet decided whether to cross the Rio Grande, which would have been an act of war, but were ostensibly searching for the bandits.

For days, the powder had been smoldering in all the men. It was Shepherd's seventeenth birthday, and he and I rode near the back. We hoped we might lay up overnight in Laredo so we could fish the Rio Grande. We had been told it held catfish large enough to swallow dogs.

We heard a shot — a surprising, unfamiliar sound, different from the tone of any of the weaponry I'd heard from our target practice — and then there was a pause, and I imagined that a gun had gone off by accident or that someone had shot at a snake or perhaps a deer. After that, there was some shouting — just a lone voice at first, but then another, and another — and then several shots together. These were answered by more shots, more shouting, and then the horses and riders around us were wheeling in different directions, some flaring away from us and others riding back past us; and my first thought was that a bear or even a jaguar was charging through our midst, within the thrashing jungle of the horses' tangled legs. Our horses were rearing and spinning, and bullets whined past. I shortened my reins, leaned into my horse, and found myself looking not for Green or Fisher but for Somervell.

I turned to shout at Shepherd and saw him get hit in the shoulder, in the meaty part just below the joint. The bullet slapped his flesh and his mouth dropped open. He was nearly tossed from his horse but only glanced at the wound, then leaned against his horse and pushed hard to rejoin me.

Somervell's men had taken cover in a line of trees on the northwestern edge of town. They climbed off their horses, reined them to branches and trunks, and then hunkered down behind logs and trees, trying to hold their fire. But a few men left their horses and ran into the fray, whooping. They disappeared into the musket smoke, waving their sabers, and were shot dead. One man, spun by the rose blossom on his chest, fell so close to me that I couldn't shake the feeling that he intercepted a bullet meant for me.

I turned and saw that Shepherd was still with me. We reached the trees and I leapt off, tied my horse to a limb, grabbed Shepherd's reins, and helped him down. The gunfire lessened, though seemed more frightening now than when the shooting had started.

"Hold your fire!" Somervell shouted. Some of his dandies still ran to join the melee and were shot — another crimson boutonniere erupting on a chest, a sudden wide birthmark on a forehead. Others were more fortunate, surviving hits by low-caliber bullets or homemade shrapnel fired from the barrel of ancient pot metal blunderbusses.

The rest of us stayed crouched and hidden. Shepherd vomited, standing upright, clutching his shoulder, blood streaming through his fingers. He walked in circles, shouting and bending over to regurgitate the morning's breakfast. He looked frightened and angry, both, and I hurried over and took him farther into the thicket, where I cleaned his shoulder with water from my canteen while he stared at me and his teeth chattered. His arms and legs began to shudder, and he looked at me in amazement and said, "I'm going to die, aren't I?"

And though I thought he might, I told him that no, he wasn't; and this calmed him so that, slowly, he stopped trembling.

The wound had a clear exit hole on the inside of his arm, just below the armpit, so there was probably no shrapnel left inside. He was bleeding heavily, and I hoped the bullet hadn't nicked an artery. I took off my shirt and bound a tight bandage, almost a tourniquet, and then sat him down under an oak tree and told him to remain still.

He was as pale as his blood was bright — there was so much of it — and we sat quietly and listened to the exchanges of gunfire and shouting. A couple of times he said, "I'm scared," but I told him to be still and hold on, that he was going to be all right; and he quieted down and clung to that advice as if I held the key to his survival. He started to shake again, and I laid my jacket across him like a blanket, and it was enough to stop his shaking.

After a while the shooting stopped — only the shouting persisted — and then there was relative silence. Not long after that, I heard our men regrouping — the burr and bray of Ewen Cameron, the occasional shouts of Green and Fisher, and the calmer declarations of Somervell — and I wanted to go and join them, but Shepherd became so pale and agitated — the crimson stains on his bandage dampening as he raised his good arm to restrain me — that I feared he would not survive my leaving, and so I stayed.

I was worried that the others might think that Shepherd and I had run away from the battle, but there was nothing I could do about that. We sat side by side beneath that oak in the failing light and listened to the sounds of our army's reassembly. It was cold — the last day of November — and as the night grew quieter, Shepherd reached for my hand and gripped it, clenching it so tightly that I thought for certain he was dying.

But he wasn't; instead, he just sat there gripping it, even as he slept. I had no matches for a fire, and no blanket with which to keep myself warm, but I did not move and tried instead to remember how warm and pleasant the day had been only hours earlier. I had almost fallen asleep in my saddle, lulled by the mild heat and the steady rocking of my horse.

We awoke later in the evening to renewed shouts, and the cries and screams of men, women, children, and horses, and dogs barking, and guns firing again. I saw by the moon that we had not slept more than an hour, but it felt that a great deal of time had passed, time not measured in minutes and hours but weighed in tons, or scaled in rods and cubits.

"Looting," Shepherd said quietly, almost wisely — as if he were the veteran of many such campaigns. His hand still gripped mine as if in lockjaw death, then released slightly.

After a while we saw reflections of firelight through the trees — how I longed to edge closer and stand beside those warming fires! — as one building after another was torched. I felt certain that these buildings, and the people that lived in them, were not the enemy: that they were merely fodder for the path of Fisher and Green, the path of history, the path of glory. And it was not I who had lit any of the torches: not a single one. What would it have hurt for me to go and warm myself beside, and benefit from, even one of them? But I could not, and so we remained back in the shadows, beyond the throw of firelight, quiet and invisible: history dust, ourselves. We heard the whoops and revelry of our own men, and their galloping horses. All through the night, people fled through the thicket, running past our spot without noticing us. Around midnight, the shouts from our men began to sound more drunken; and not much after that, musical instruments began to play — horns and fifes and guitars — a mock-joyful symphony issuing from the burning town.

A fiddle was found, though no true fiddler, for the sounds that emanated from those tortured strings were dirgelike and anguished; and from elsewhere in the village there came random and occasional drumming — stones against overturned empty barrels, wooden clubs against the sides of buildings, musket butts against doorways — and more laughter and revelry, more cries of fright.

If we slept again at all, we might have done so for a few moments just before the cold dawn. Then, only because we had no more water, and because James Shepherd felt that he would die of thirst without some, he allowed me to leave the grasp of his hand and venture into the village to get water and to take stock of what had happened.

"If they capture you," he said, "don't leave me here. Make them come get me."

His arm was hurting terribly, all soft-tissue tear, without a bone broken — and I told him not to be ridiculous, that I couldn't be captured because they were on my side and I was on theirs. But he just looked at me, understanding what I didn't. I have no idea how two boys growing up in the same small town could know such disparate things and, in the end, turn out so differently.

Corrals and barns stood empty, their gates and doors demolished. Low fires smoldered and crackled almost every-where I looked. A mist was beginning to fall, mingling smoke with the morning's fog, and I smelled not only the charred odor of wood but other things not meant to burn — a scent of trash, like spoiled fruit, and burning metal, and wet cloth.

There were dead animals everywhere — dogs and chick-ens strewn in the street, with a layer of dust absorbing the morning's mist and slowly transforming to mud. There were dead horses and cattle, mules and pigs, too, some shot and others killed by swords.

Murdered men and women lay in the street, too, their congealed blood loosened in the light rain. Scraps and rags of clothing lay the streets, a man hung from a second-story balcony, a crude noose around his neck, his head and arms drooping.

In the gray light, I saw that some of the outstretched bod-ies were stirring. A man tried to sit up, put his hands to his head, then tipped over on his side. A woman with a battered face reached down to pull her shawl up farther over her and then lay looking up into the rain.

I didn't know whom to help or where to turn; there was too much carnage. I found a bloodless severed hand in the street — a woman's? A young man's? — and walked past it, puking bile. I would find water for James Shepherd and then go back to him. And after that, we would return home and start over. Our quiet lives would be enough.

I understood that I was looking into some horrific new territory that could never be forgotten, and more than any-thing I wanted to flee, even abandoning Shepherd, but I stepped over and around carcasses and went up the stairs of the only building left unharmed. The downstairs was some sort of lobby. I ascended to the second floor and saw why the building was unscathed. Green and Fisher had commandeered it for their headquarters — Wallace was there, too, and half a dozen others whose looks were terrifying.

They sat in a circle of mismatched chairs. Green and Somervell's chairs were turned backwards so that they straddled them like horses. They leaned forward in the chairs, resting the weight of their torsos against the backs, as if even here they intended to somehow charge into battle. Of them all, only Fisher seemed relaxed, with one leg stretched out before him. All of the men's boots and pants were wet, and a dull fire in the stove was only now beginning to warm enough to send up steam.

Empty whiskey bottles lay on the floor, and several men held partly finished tumblers, though while I was there, none of them drank, as if, finally, they'd had enough.

Ashy-faced, nearly all were smoking, a raft of blue smoke hanging halfway to the ceiling. They looked at me with a mix of curiosity and hostility. I wondered if any of them had hung the man across the street, and for what offense.

There was a little sound from outside on the porch, a kind of a hiss or gasp, like the air going out of something — the sound of an injured man or woman dying — and the men gave no indication of noticing. After a moment, I eased out of the room and went back downstairs.

Outside, a raven filtered down from the fog and smoke and settled onto the shoulder of one of the fallen, as if that man were his master and the raven had been seeking him out, returning after a long night's absence. The raven perched for a moment, clutching the man's stiff shoulder as if waiting for him to awaken, and, when he did not, the raven edged a couple of hops closer to the man's clenched face, and with a delicate motion of his heavy bill, pulled the lids open and daintily pecked his eyes.

I hurried out into the street and shooed the raven away. I walked closer to the man and saw a crumpled trumpet lying in the mud next to him. I looked up and saw across the street, in the downstairs doorway of the building from which the hanged man was suspended, a young child watching, barely a toddler. I went back to the sidewalk and picked up several of the empty whiskey bottles, filled them from a watering trough, and hurried off, three clinking bottles in each arm.

Knowing Shepherd's sensitive nature, his queasiness regarding blood and pain and entrails, I wasn't sure I should tell him what I'd seen. I came hurrying down the trail through the thicket and found him awake and watching for me. He had been crying, and little rivers and deltas of salt tracked the dust and grime on his face. He asked what took me so long, and I told him that, yes, there had been looting.

He greedily drank the water. His arm was so swollen that he could barely move it, and I was about to examine it when Fisher came galloping down the narrow trail, brush thwacking his small agile horse at every turn, so that Fisher seemed barely in control.

He reined to a slashing stop, spraying a shower of sand across us. At first I didn't understand that he had come after me. I thought the rage in his eyes was about his horse's behavior, or that he was chasing someone else — some bandit, some infidel to the republic.

He leapt down from his horse, one hand on the reins and

the other on his sword. He glanced at Shepherd and then at me.

"What is your intent?" Fisher demanded, glancing possessively at Shepherd, believing perhaps that I had kidnapped him and would form a splintered ragtag militia of two. Fisher gripped the butt of his sword. "Just where did you think you were going?" he asked. "We can't be having desertions. The mission hasn't even begun." He gestured toward town.

"My friend is hurt," I answered. "I'm taking care of him."

Then Fisher went to Shepherd and held his arm almost tenderly and examined the blood-soaked bandage with a critical and scornful but concerned air.

"May I look at it?" he asked.

The wound hurt and Shepherd could barely tolerate the lightest touch, but he didn't protest while Fisher touched the wound with his long fingers, then traced the blood-streaked tracks of impending infection.

Sweat beaded around Shepherd's scalp and trickled down his nose and fell in splattering drops. Fisher studied upon the wound almost admiringly.

"Another inch to the left or the right, and you'd be as dead as the ones we left behind," Fisher said. "Still, you're not out of it. We'll have to get this dressed." He looked up at me inquiringly and then remembered who I was — he did not need my permission — and he gestured for one of the whiskey bottles of water.

Taking a rumpled, dirty handkerchief from his coat pocket, he dabbed the water onto it. At the first firm touch, Shepherd's eyes sought mine, wildly, as if pleading, and Fisher tensed. Shepherd bit his lip and didn't cry out, but simply shuddered, and Fisher relaxed and went on cleaning the wound.

Soon I untied the horses and held Shepherd's as Fisher helped him into the saddle. I felt I was betraying him, sending him off to his doom.

We rode the brushy trail back into the clearing where the fighting had begun. We saw dead horses, dead villagers, dead Texans. Our horses shied, and Shepherd glanced at me, starting to understand, I think, that we were traveling in the wrong direction.

I followed them at a distance. James Shepherd, never a good rider, listed in his saddle, unable to lift his damaged arm. Fisher rode on his bad side to catch him should he fall.

In Laredo, Somervell and his men were cleaning the streets. In the daylight hours, I had seldom seen him dismounted. He walked bandy-legged along with several of his men, gathering torn, ragged garments from mud puddles, carrying armloads of them like washerwomen, and dragging corpses off the streets and leaning them against the sides of buildings, their heads down-tipped and shoulders slumped, as if they were only napping.

When we came to the hotel in which the officers had gathered that morning, a fire burned in the middle of the street, with half a hundred men gathered around. I smelled meat cooking and saw that the men were roasting several pigs.

Fisher dismounted and helped Shepherd dismount. He handed me their reins to hitch their horses and gestured Shepherd to precede him up the stairs. When I followed, Fisher turned and I thought he was going to tell me to remain downstairs, but he said nothing.

Upstairs, he sat down with Green and the others, and then Somervell came up the steps, angry, and informed Green and Fisher that he was taking his men north and disbanding them, that this regiment was a disgrace to the republic.

Fisher's face darkened and he rose with his hand on his sword, half-drawn, but Green intervened by firing his pistol into the floor.

Green's volley was answered by the whoops and shouts of the soldiers down by the pig roast — they started firing their own weapons — and after a moment of cold staring between Somervell and Fisher, Somervell turned and went back toward the stairs to gather his men and leave. I knew I should go with him.

Somervell was two paces away, and then he was three and four. Even at five and then six paces there was time. And how would my life have been different, if I had left? The difference was not along a fine line or in a shade of gray. It was a stark and enormous abyss.

We had a feast, and after the last of the pigs were eaten, along with a great iron kettle of hominy, seasoned with chili peppers and dotted with flecks of ash from the fire, we bid farewell to the terrorized town, Green and Fisher vowing loudly to whoever might be within hearing that we would return and erase Laredo from the face of the earth if we were fired upon again and that the same would hold true for any other village along the border.

Shepherd rode at the front, next to Fisher, and wore an expression of foolish pride. I remembered what Green's face looked like when the shooting started: how eager he had looked, and how instantaneous the change had been. As if he had been listening for that one sound all along. He was in his mid-thirties — twice my age — and had seen war, and had become not just accustomed to it, but something more.

I think that Lieutenant Somervell loved war, too — a harsh word, *loved*, but I think the only one for it — but loved it so much that he could not tolerate what had happened at Laredo and the way his men had behaved, in their sack and plunder. I think he loved war so much that he was truly surprised that it had turned out that way.

It was here, at the feast — the ruined town still cowering as we celebrated in the street — that Somervell announced his intent to turn back, to return home with his men, numbering nearly a hundred, while they still could. And it was here where we learned the unspoken contents of the letter that Green had been reading to us.

Fisher had seen the letter, as had Somervell. Only they knew its entire contents. Somervell, a learned man, knew it well enough to quote it by heart: as if in the days preceding the debacle at Laredo and then the hours following he had been pondering it.

"You will be controlled by only the most civilized warfare, and you will find great advantage of exercising great humanity towards the common people." He said nothing more, but rose and mounted his mud-caked horse, called his men into formation, and left, riding back north: and I think that I was not the only one who wanted to go with them.

"He cracked," Fisher said reflectively, after they were gone, seeming completely unconcerned by our diminishment. "I've seen it before. You never know who will crack."

I looked over at Green, my captain, expecting him to disparage Somervell also. But Green said nothing, was only staring down at the coffee mug he held in both hands.

We wandered for nearly three weeks up and down the river, no longer searching for bandits but daily reminded by Fisher and Green of the importance of the great new country claimed from Mexico, by the blood spent at the Alamo and San Jacinto, and how much the Mexicans wanted Texas back.

In each village on our side of the river we found Texans and Mexicans living, all speaking Spanish. The fear in their eyes said that they'd heard of the atrocities at Laredo. They greeted us with great masks of hospitality — *Buenos dias, señores caballeros; nos gustan mucho los Americanos. Bienvenidos, estranjeros! Beinvenidos!* Good day, gentlemen; we like the Americans very much. Welcome, strangers, welcome!

No longer were banquets prepared in our honor, but the villagers offered dried fruits, vegetables, beef, and other stock, and during the next month we patrolled the border for days at a time, searching for war, until we wore ourselves ragged and hungry and returned to one of the villages we claimed to defend, where we received provisions. Then we pressed back on into the wilderness.

Shepherd's arm was deteriorating. We had a surgeon along, a Dr. Sinnickson, who treated numerous men with mercury following the soiree at Laredo, fearing the onset of syphilis. He tended to Shepherd's arm, cleaning it and dousing it with alcohol, saying that the cooler weather of December would serve him well, and that had he received the wound in midsummer, insects would have immediately found it.

The insects found it anyway, and the arm began to swell with an odor now so ripe that all of the men could smell it. We talked about whether it would have to be amputated.

But Shepherd blossomed in his position at the front of the line. Green and Fisher, disparate yet as conjoined as sun and moon, continued to flank either side of the column, and Shepherd shadowed, and was shadowed by, Fisher at almost every turn.

Shepherd didn't ignore me but didn't petition me to join him up front. He was growing away from me, yet I kept him in sight, if only to be able to report back to his family.

Occasionally, after taking his dinner with the officers, Shepherd rode over to whichever fire I was seated at, ostensibly to check on me. His horsemanship had improved, as had his self-assurance, and when he sat with me for a few minutes, he filled me in on how his life was changing.

He slept in the officers' tent with Fisher and his aide, Henry Franklin. Fisher was teaching him military strategy, he said. He was eager for battle, though I saw the old fear in him, rivaling his desire.

I wanted no special recognition from Green or Fisher but envied Shepherd's ease and power.

"How's your arm?" I asked.

"It hurts," he admitted. He knew about the wagering on whether or not the arm would be amputated, yet seemed not to care, seemed almost exultant.

"What do you think about this big river?" I asked. The Rio Grande was almost always in sight. "Do you think we could fish it one night?"

"I want to cross that damn river," he said. "Captain Fisher does, too." He spit. "Green doesn't."

His arm smelled like rot, and a few minutes later, when Fisher came riding up, looking angry, and Shepherd rose quickly and left, I was glad.

Orlando Phelps, another man at the fire — only a year older than I and small and dark-skinned, with a Mexican mother — watched the two men ride away and laughed. "I see that your friend has become frail." He said it without cruelty or taunt but in surprised observation. He started to ask me something but let it drop. And for myself, I couldn't think how to approach the question of James Shepherd. What was the source of his anger? It was carrying him away.

Up and down the river we patrolled, quarreling among ourselves, Ewen Cameron sometimes the instigator and other times the peacemaker, able single-handedly to subdue three or four men. I fell in with a group of boys — John Hill, Jesse Yocum, Orlando Phelps, Billy Reese, Gilbert Brush, and Harvey Sellers, most of whom were fourteen or fifteen. We watched the junior officers jockeying and plotting, with scrapes becoming increasingly frequent around each night's campfire, though the next day always brought renewed solidarity.

The weather grew colder and rainy, our bellies gaunt and our clothes shabby. Captain Green's letter was tattered nearly to pieces now, and our fiddles had all been lost or left behind.

Orlando Phelps and I and the other boys fished in the evenings. In the deepest pools of the Rio Grande there were catfish far bigger than anything ever hauled out of the James. For bait, we used the cut-up shanks of deer legs, ladled from our evening stew, or the offal of javelinas, or rabbits, or small birds. The catfish were always hungry, and there were endless numbers of them.

Seated by a fire on the riverbank, we each baited a big hook, tossed our lines in, and waited. We talked about home, and what we'd do when we got back. John Hill was particularly homesick and spoke often of his younger brothers and sisters. "There's this big tree we liked to all climb," he said, and then corrected himself. "This tree we *like* to climb. You can see all the way to the Brazos. It's a cool place in the summer. We would all five climb up in that tree and nap like coons, in the breeze, when we had our chores done."

A ferocious splashing commenced out in the river, a shout came from one of the boys, and then there was a sound like a cow trying to swim the river. And all the cheers and curses that went up would surely have alerted any soldiers on the Mexican side. The boys got the fish up on the bank, and clubbed it before it could break the line and slither back into the river.

Gasping, flopping, writhing in the sand, the fish looked half as large as a calf. We caught several every evening, but it wasn't the same as with James Shepherd before the war. It was satisfying but not pleasant.

Some of the catfish were so big they broke the line and took our hooks, and when we lost all our hooks, we whittled new ones from green mesquite and huisache. Every evening we landed two or three dragonlike monsters and were proud to help provision the straggling army.

Henry Whaling, a large youth of eighteen, busied himself catching smaller fish in the shallows, using crickets for bait. His fish were little larger than sardines, too small to bother dragging back to camp, so he made his own fire in the sand by the river and cooked them on a stick and ate them as fast as he caught them, a dozen or sometimes two in an evening.

On such nights, war seemed far away and almost forgotten. The next day on the trail, many of us could barely stay awake. Lulled by the jingle of the horses' bits and the ship-like creak of old leather, we kept falling asleep in our saddles. We would lurch back into wakefulness just in time to keep from falling from our horses. And it seemed that as we napped, we traveled to some deep, wonderful place, from which we emerged refreshed, even gilded; and shaking our heads to clear them from the dreamy residue of that brief voyage, we took the reins in both hands and nudged our horses into a trot, hurrying to catch up.

One evening, after we set up camp, we heard a single shot, not from across the border but from behind us. Thinking we were being fired upon, we scrambled onto our horses, leaving our cooking fires and extra stock untended, and charged off into the brush under the semicommand of scattered officers.

But what we found was fifteen-year-old John Hill, huddled crying over the body of his fourteen-year-old friend Jesse Yocum.

They'd been out rabbit hunting, crawling through the brush, and a branch snagged the trigger of Hill's gun, discharging a bullet into Yocum's back. Hill hurried to Yocum, turned him over, and saw a gaping exit wound in his ribs. Yocum barely had time to forgive Hill before he died.

We carried the body back to camp and wrapped it in blankets to prepare it for burial the next day. All that night, the camp was kept awake by Hill's sobbing.

In the morning, under a cold rain with a northwest wind, we buried Yocum in an unmarked grave on a bluff of the Rio Grande, Yocum's head slightly elevated and his boots pointing north into the republic younger than himself.

Shepherd's arm was the next thing lost. Some days we smelled it from a distance, and other days there was little scent at all. At times, the flesh of his arm was putrescent, bruised and streaked with rivulets of blood and pus, grit and debris. Nightly, Shepherd yelled as Dr. Sinnickson attempted to irrigate the wound, though each day the wind brought new dust and dirt. Sometimes it seemed to have sealed over with a vitreous, almost metallic sheen, and on those days the odor was subdued, and we could hope that beneath the fiery purple scab, the flesh was knitting.

Some days even his breath was gangrenous, and I thought we might lose him yet. Instead, three days after we buried Yocum, Shepherd lost the arm. Sinnickson had been preparing him for the eventuality, but Shepherd had been resisting it. The issue resolved itself when Shepherd passed out while riding. He landed on his bad arm, rupturing it. Pulpy fragments remained on the rocks where he fell. The arm was bleeding profusely, and Sinnickson tied it off.

A tent was set up. Sinnickson directed Shepherd to drink three glasses of whiskey, while we built a low fire in the rain, in order to boil the carving knives and fine-toothed saw he carried in his satchel. They tied Shepherd down, with Cameron's help.

While Shepherd screamed and cursed — before he passed out — Sinnickson sawed the arm off through the top of the shoulder, as if quartering a deer, taking a piece of the shoulder, clamping the artery with horsehair thread and then cauterizing the flesh before sewing the flap of bruised skin back over the wound. He told us the gangrene was close to Shepherd's heart and gave him a one in ten chance of surviving, but he did not say this to Shepherd.

Captain Fisher wrapped the arm in a sheet and grabbed me by my arm, and we stumbled off into the rain, toward the officer's latrine, where he got a shovel and thrust it at me. Then we reeled off into the brush, down toward the river.

I dug, while Fisher knelt clutching the arm. The soil was sandy and soft in the rain, and soon I had a pit deep enough to bury a body in. He handed me the arm and watched as I laid it in the sand, climbed out, and shoveled sand over it. We stood by the mound until finally Fisher fetched a large rounded stone from the bluff and placed it on the mound as a marker.

We went back to the tent, where Shepherd lay unconscious. Fisher, Sinnickson, and I sat waiting for Shepherd to come to, and I wondered if I might be asked to ride up front, and whether I wanted to. Sometime after midnight, Shepherd awoke wailing and thrashing in pain. We struggled to hold him down, Shepherd cursing us, Mexicans, war, God, his family, and all the world. Fisher's aide, Franklin, ran to get the big Scot, Ewen Cameron, to help hold Shepherd down again, while others tied rope and strips of bed sheet around him.

For nearly two hours, Shepherd carried on so loudly that wolves and coyotes answered with their own wails. Finally he fell unconscious. I wanted to stay there in the tent with him, but Fisher told me to go get some rest.

No one in camp believed that Shepherd would survive the

night. Money changed hands, wagers made on his demise in terms not of if but when. My campmates' voices fell when I approached. "Is he living?" Billy Reese asked, just a boy himself. "Is he alive?" I said that he was, and that he was going to survive and live a full, useful life, doing many great things. The men and boys paused, then resumed their wagering.

We stayed in camp for five days while Shepherd's shoulder healed, Sinnickson administering laudanum in scrimping doses, and only when Fisher ordered him to. Shepherd slept and was semiconscious most of the time. His waking moments were highlighted by screams and curses, making not just the men but even the horses in their hobbles nervous, and frightening the nearby game, so that our hunters had to travel farther to find success.

The boys and I fished each evening and napped during the day, wrapped in our blankets under scraggly mesquite trees, with the stark December sun on our faces. Several times each day I checked on Shepherd. On occasion, he was awake and not howling but silent and grim-faced. He looked ten years older and fierce. He wanted to know what we had done with the arm and if I was certain that it hadn't been salvageable. As if he were considering returning to it, or returning to something. The boy he had been, perhaps.

Meanwhile, the tension grew between Green and Fisher. Green wanted to move on, whether Shepherd was ready or not. Sinnickson said Shepherd would benefit from another week of rest, but Shepherd was antsy to travel again.

I wondered where Somervell was by now. It was a few days before Christmas, and what I wanted was a fine Christmas feast at home with my family. But most of the men were anxious to forge south, which was more perplexing when I learned that Green and many of his men, including Cameron and Wallace, had been captured by the Mexicans before, while they were under the command of Zachary Taylor.

Green and several hundred of his men had been scheduled for execution until they vowed, under penalty of death, never to take up arms against Mexico again and never even to venture back into Mexico. (Under much these same terms, Santa Anna was allowed to return to Mexico after his defeat at San Jacinto. Some said he retired and was living on the coast in Vera Cruz, raising fighting cocks and tending a garden of orchids, while others said he was plotting a return and had been a secret partner in General Woll's raids on San Antonio.) Whatever pact Green and his men had made, they were ready, less than a year later, to betray it.

Aggression mounted, the turmoil in our spirits agitated by the delay, the cold wet weather, and the increasing squalor of camp. There were more fights, until finally the situation grew so untenable that Fisher agreed we had to move, whether Shepherd was ready or not. Fisher planned to leave me and his aide, Franklin, with Shepherd, with instructions to catch up as soon as Shepherd could travel; but on the morning of the sixth day, as the men broke camp, rolling up wet tents and unhobbling the stock, Shepherd asked Franklin to saddle his horse, and then climbed up onto it and declared himself ready.

He didn't look graceful, hauling himself up onto that horse. Shepherd's legs, never powerful, were weak from his ordeal, and he nearly fell backwards. Franklin hovered to catch him, but once he was up, he sat with a certain nobility. The men gave a great cheer, Fisher looked overcome with pride, and we moved out, Shepherd in the lead between Fisher and Green, the ranks behind them serpentine, disjointed, rusty, but rested. Ready to kill and be killed.

The weather grew worse — fog and cold mist that turned to sleet. Icicles hung from our horses' nostrils and the brims of our hats. Our rations and clothes were worse than ever, but our spirits received a boost when, in a steady downpour, Henry Whaling, Billy Reese, and I glimpsed the horrific and exhilarating sight of the Mexican army moving through the fog at dusk on the other side of the river, heading upstream toward Laredo. It was but blind luck that we weren't already on the riverbank, fishing, but in the bushes, where we remained, watching and taking a rough assay of their numbers. We counted two thousand before darkness obscured the columns. If they were searching for us, we were flattered and terrified that we were considered dangerous enough to inspire such a large expedition. At camp, we announced our discovery, and after a quick parley, Green and Fisher decided to push hard upstream and cross the river a day or two ahead of the Mexicans' march. There we would capture and hold hostage the first undefended village we found.

I knew it was wrong. The logic was obviously faulty, but I had been stirred by the sight of the Mexican cavalry, the precision of their riverside march. It was an honor to be their enemy. Green encouraged us, "You may take pride in the battle when the cause is just." When I asked myself much later why he and Fisher had not turned back north to recruit more men to fill Somervell's departure, it occurred to me that they were afraid they would be disciplined for the atrocities in Laredo. That already, they — we — were prisoners.

In a long and tattered line, our horses slick and darkened by the cold rain, we rode without lanterns through the night. All I saw in front of me were milky clouds of breath from my horse and plumes from the horse ahead.

We prepared to cross over near the Mexican village of Guerrero, which would be our first target. We didn't go fishing that night but stayed around our campfires, cleaning and re-cleaning our weapons and talking quietly. Bigfoot Wallace argued with old Ezekiel Smith about the relative unimportance of numbers in opposing armies. In a cause such as ours, Wallace argued, we could succeed with one tenth the force of our enemy. A discussion ensued concerning which was the greater war — Thermopylae, under the defense of Leonidas I, or our own recent Alamo, in which one hundred and eighty-six men stood against six thousand of Santa Anna's finest, buying time and inflicting enough casualties to allow Sam Houston his victory at San Jacinto a month later. Ezekiel Smith held that Thermopylae was the greater victory, since it allowed Greece to become Greece, whereas the birth of Texas meant nothing to the world. Wallace disagreed strongly, promising that the republic was a cradle of democracy, the birthplace of a civilization that would advance arts and letters, science, engineering, the production of goods from a bounty of natural resources, and, above all, the chivalry, honesty, fortitude, and fairness that marked man's highest purpose. He became so exercised in his assertions that I think he would have thrashed the old man had Smith dared to disagree.

*   *   *

We crossed the river in the darkness before first light, riding into Guerrero in a heavy downpour. The smoke from the pueblos hung dense and blue. We were agitated, nervous that the slightest sound would give us away, unleashing enemy fire. The creak of saddle leather from so many horses and the splashing surge of our river crossing swept me up in a collective courage and daring. I was not afraid of dying, only losing.

We rode into the darkened village with our rifles ready, our pistols loaded. Those of us who carried swords had practiced drawing them, for use in close combat. We entered the village and rode through it, nearly a thousand horse hooves clopping, a sound from a dream perhaps. A few dogs roused and barked. I was certain we would find our battle, and waited in delighted anticipation for the first rifle shot.

We rode all the way through the village undisturbed, then turned around and came back to its center. Fisher and Green dismounted and announced loudly to the sleeping town that we would now be occupying it, holding it hostage. The rest of us sat on our horses, strung out up and down the streets, while Fisher and Green dispatched a number of men to commandeer enemy funds.

We took possession of the village without a single shot being fired; indeed, we never saw a weapon in Guerrero other than our own. The inhabitants were gaunt mules and starving paisanos. *Hostage to what?* one of them asked.

Fisher found the town priest and threatened to harm him if a $5,000 ransom was not paid. He gestured toward Shepherd and indicated that with his good arm Shepherd would execute the priest with a sword.

The town leaders hurried from door to door in the driving rain — curious faces appearing in the open doorways and windows while we sat around on our horses getting drenched. The town presented us with $381 at noon, and after counting it Green spat and said, "If that's all they can do, tell them to keep it."

We stayed the night, splitting up and taking refuge in the huts of the starving villagers, with none of the revelry of Laredo; as if, to a man, we were ashamed of that past behavior, and as if the spirit of Christmas commanded us, in spite of Fisher's threats to the priest. The rain shifted to sleet. We shared soup with the various families whose huts we occupied.

In the morning, we discovered that many of the lame and starving of our horses had died from the freezing cold. After we butchered and ate as much as we could hold, there was horse meat left for the villagers, and they asked for the hides of the horses as well.

Two more of our lieutenants — Byrd and Kenedy — decided to turn back, taking their men with them. Several men not belonging to the two lieutenants' companies chose to go with them. One man — Joseph Berry — was suffering from a cactus needle lodged in his leg, his kneecap stinking and swelling, Sinnickson eyeing it daily — but Berry chose to stay.

Fisher, however, was determined to push south — *Look how easily Guerrero fell*, he argued. *Why not continue southward, and achieve even greater victory?*

He and Green both scowled after these newest defectors, but being an unofficial army — more marauders than militia — neither had any true military authority, and with each passing defection they were reminded of this.

That afternoon we rode toward the little town of Ciudad Mier, where, that evening, we again took a priest hostage, demanding ransom before retiring to our ragged camp back in the brush. Fisher told the townspeople that they had forty-eight hours to deliver the ransom — ten thousand dollars, this time, to make up for the inadequacy of Guerrero — and that he would meet them on the bank of the Rio Grande on Christmas Eve Day.

I was part of the detail charged with guarding the priest, who seemed affable and forgiving. A lean man in his mid-fifties, he told us stories of saints and sinners he had known in his life. Men and women who had been little better than pagans, he said, as prone to pray to the animals of the fields and forests as to the highest of gods. Men and women who prayed to the weather, or the bare stone of the desert; or, worse yet, he said, who prayed not at all, but who instead assumed that all matters concerning their needs as well as their desires had been prearranged. He spoke to us partly in English and partly in Spanish, with Alfred Thurmond helping translate.

"There was one such man," he said, "one who believed his destiny was laid before him like a gleaming road, and who believed he could pass through danger unharmed, like a man — a circus master passing through a crowd of lions or tigers. Jaguars," the priest said, "and *panteras*.

"He could be said to be a good man, in that he concerned himself with the welfare of others less fortunate than himself, and the welfare of the village — but he did not believe that his life was built of choices. Did not believe that he was the mason, constructing it with each hour of his life, and each day.

"We argued often about this. Of course to such a man, prayer was unknown: there was no need for it. He simply followed his life. This man was a farmer," the priest said, "and it was a source of frustration to the rest of us, and to the other farmers who worked so hard, that this man's crops were always more bountiful than the other farmers' in hard seasons, though this man, Pico, never troubled himself overmuch with his labors. *Un medio,*" the priest said, and one of our men clarified the interpretation, calling out "A half-ass," and the priest shrugged, then nodded.

"I asked him to become a man of God," the priest said. "I asked him to consider that many things in the world were undecided, things in which a strong and fiery heart could make a difference. Desperate things in need of salvation," the priest said. "But Pico always shook his head and said that I was wrong.

"He ate and drank as he wished, philandered as he wished — his wife abandoned him — and yet, as I said, nothing mattered much to him. His heart was not afire; it could be neither changed nor harmed. If someone asked him for a favor — anything — he would do it — but he passed through his years like a sleepwalker. He smiled, joked, sang, worked. But he was asleep. I was the only one who knew it. Again and again, I tried to awaken him, but I could not." The priest shook his head and looked down at his hands sorrowfully. As if the man had been his own brother.

"What happened to him?" I asked. "Is he still alive?"

The priest looked up and smiled at my interest. "I do not know," he said. "I think that maybe he just went away. He vanished. We stopped seeing him, and no one knew what had become of him. It was as if he never was."

But Pico was not the worst, the priest said. Most distressing of all to him, he said, were those who waited until the end to pray. He glanced around at us as if in secret commiseration rather than indictment. As if we already were, and always had been, men of God, to whom he could speak frankly about such things.

Certainly, the priest said, as a man of God himself, he welcomed the opportunity to receive the souls of those whose hearts changed in the last days, and the last hour, but it saddened him deeply, he said, to consider all the wasted time behind such last-minute conversions — the backwash, he called it, the rubble of compassion whose seeds never germinated, the toxic residue of a lifetime of ill deeds.

The priest had seen much waste in his lifetime, he told us, and much loneliness, and to him, the loneliness was the worst thing of all.

On Christmas Eve Day, Fisher took a detail to the riverbank to collect the ransom. Shepherd rode with him, so hard-faced, and looking so much older, that I barely recognized him, and when he turned to look back at camp before riding off, he looked right through me, not with anger or hostility or envy or sadness, but simply through me, as if one of us had already left this world.

"A friend of yours?" the priest asked, observing the strange moment.

I took a long time answering. "Yes," I said finally.

He resumed his narrative about the streets and palaces in the kingdom of heaven — how such an architecture in the hearts of men and women and children gave way to the creation and construction of a similar architecture in the physical world, which those dreamers and initiates could then inhabit. He believed that a paucity of such compassion led to the construction of a life, and a landscape, of the destitute.

He looked around at us, and I felt he was reading our faces and fates as clearly as if he had unscrolled the map of a much-traveled country, as if he could see as well the country through which we had already traveled.

He did not seem troubled by his situation with us. He seemed prepared to live or die — accepting either with dignity — and it was this quality that kept us clustered around him.

We waited all morning and into the afternoon for Fisher and his men to return. The priest appeared unfazed, though later in the day he asked if he could have a little privacy in a tent, so we fastened a leash to his wrists and ankles and allowed him to go into the tent by himself, where he stayed for a good two hours. We assumed he was praying, though when I went in to take him some fish soup at dinner, I found that he was sound asleep, lying on the ground on his back with his hands clasped and folded neatly over his chest.

He opened his eyes, sat up, and after a moment inquired about Joseph Berry's knee — asking how long it had been infected and how he had injured it — and said that he had offered up a prayer on Joseph Berry's behalf.

Fisher and his regiment didn't get back until shortly after

dark, having waited on the riverbank all day to no avail: they left two men there overnight, in case the ransom was merely running late. They had discussed going back into town but feared a trap.

That night, they ordered that the priest not be given any food — as if by punishing him in secret the ransom seekers might somehow, through divine intuition, be inspired to search harder for the ransom, or as if the priest, with his allotted hours expired, were living on borrowed time.

The priest was quieter, that last night. Those of us who were guarding him sought to assure him that we were certain the ransom would be delivered the next day, but he remained courteous though distant and, finally, with our permission, bid us good night. Shackled, he crawled into his tent, and after a little while we heard him snoring.

We went to bed not long after that, save for the lookouts. It was the quietest and strangest Christmas Eve I have ever known. I think that each of us was considering the priest's plight.

The next day, Christmas, we had a short prayer, officiated by Sinnickson, who had also been a preacher for a while. I sat next to Shepherd and watched how he labored to cut his dried mutton with his knife before he finally gave up, picking it up with his free hand and gnawing on it, as many of the nonofficers did.

Otherwise, Shepherd held himself like an officer, with an erect, guarded posture, and dressed like an officer, in one of Fisher's coats with the sleeve pinned, and sat his horse like an officer, and carried an officer's sword. But he gnawed on that mutton like the most savage of us — like Bigfoot Wallace himself, or even the brute Cameron. When he saw me watching him, he scowled and stared at me with such steel that I felt we had become enemies.

We finished our thin rations, and Fisher and his men were about to ride back down to the river to wait again for the ransom when a lone Mexican sheepherder came walking into camp, unarmed.

We were antsy, and some of the irregulars who first spied the sheepherder nearly cut him down with their muskets and pistols; but the sheepherder raised his hands carefully, and they allowed him to come all the way into camp.

He said that no one had sent him, but that he had come on his own, out of concern for the priest and as a gesture of goodwill as well to the Texans, to let us know that two of Mexico's fiercest commanders, General Pedro de Ampudia and General Antonio Canales, had arrived in Ciudad Mier less than a day after the priest was taken hostage. Ampudia and Canales were commanding nearly a thousand men, the sheepherder said, and they had instructed the town not to pay the ransom.

Fisher cursed and leapt up, spilling his coffee and burning himself, and, in a rage, ordered the sheepherder to be taken hostage too. Green and Fisher's aides complied, binding the sheepherder's wrists and ankles with rope before leading him to the priest's tent, where the priest welcomed him like a lost brother.

There followed a brief and heated counsel, unique in that the soldiers were included. The reason for this, as well as for Fisher's agitation, was that many of our men had once ridden with Canales. Canales, who had renounced his Mexican citizenship, had been a soldier in the Texas army — a mercenary, and a fierce one at that. He and many of the men among us had fought against General Ampudia, who never renounced his homeland.

Ampudia, the men said, was fiercer than Canales. In one battle, back in Texas, when the two men opposed each other, Ampudia captured one of Canales's fellow insurrectionists and decapitated him, boiled his head in a vat of grease, and stuck it on a pike in front of the man's home. That Ampudia and Canales had joined forces set off new currents of alternating fear and bravado in the camp — the fear hidden, the bravado manifest.

Green convinced Fisher that we should take a vote on whether to engage Ampudia and Canales, capture the town of Mier, and then continue south, looting and raising more funds — or whether we should turn back. Fisher hesitated, ill at ease with any notion of democracy within the military ranks, but his rage had subsided enough for him to see the reason behind Green's proposal. A militia that determined its own fate would be more committed going into battle, and we would need every bit of ferocity and valor we could muster.

The men voted almost unanimously to attack — about twenty men abstained, and another small group counseled that we wait for a more propitious time, though after the vote the naysayers and the abstainers allowed themselves to be carried with the group. The vote had whipped the men into a frenzy. They believed that even if Ampudia and Canales commanded six thousand, our expedition could handle them. Fisher expressed the deepest regret about the need to execute the priest and the sheepherder. Fisher explained it to the men, and then, in heartfelt words, explained it also to the priest and sheepherder, admonishing the villains Ampudia and Canales for abandoning the priest.

Fisher instructed his aide to take the two out into the brush and bind them to a tree, and he assigned Shepherd to fire the shots. A small group, including Fisher, took the priest and sheepherder, shackled and bound, hobbling into the brush. Shepherd walked beside Fisher with his chin up and his eyes forward, seeming to take no notice of the priest and sheepherder.

The priest looked around him and his eyes fell on me. *"Vayan con Dios,"* he said softly, *"soldados desgraciados."* And then he and the others continued on into the brush. A short while later, we heard one gunshot and then the second.

Fisher and Shepherd came walking out of the brush — the others remained behind to do the burying and to construct crude crosses — and I could not help but notice that Fisher looked pleased: as if Shepherd had performed exactly as Fisher wished, with no weakness or hesitation.

We spent the afternoon huddled in the rain, planning our attack, sending out scouts and then conferring with them, checking and rechecking our weapons and imagining all the different ways to kill the enemy.

At the time, our plan seemed to me bold and elegant. Canales had stationed some of his men around the northern perimeter of the town, ostensibly to defend it but possibly to lure us to fight there. Fisher, having fought him before, suspected that if we fought Canales on the perimeter, he would retreat into the core of Mier, where Ampudia's larger force and the rest of Canales's men would be waiting. The Mexicans were lovers of pageantry, he said, and Green concurred; the Mexicans in the town would be lined up in cavalry formations, waiting to be stirred to action by the shrilling of trumpets. In light of this knowledge, it was decided that when Canales's men on the perimeter turned and fled, we would pursue them into Mier, pretending not to know it was a trap, but we would not pursue them to the center of the town. Instead, we'd commandeer some of the adobe homes. They were built shoulder to shoulder, and we could use them to stand our ground or could move slowly forward by knocking out the wall of one adobe and rushing into the next one — gnawing our way through the town, as Fisher described it — and, in the end, after we killed all of Canales's and Ampudia's troops, we would also have leveled the town, and it would serve as an example to other villages not to resist our advance.

I looked over at Green and his aide to see how they were taking Fisher's plan. Green was pale and listless, unlike his usual confrontational, swaggering self.

"We will crush them," Fisher said. "We will destroy them. We will annihilate them, we will lay waste to everything they ever owned as punishment for having resisted us earlier, when we were moderate. They will wish forever that they had listened to us rather than having opposed us, and when we are done, we will find the treasures they sought to keep hidden."

We waited in the freezing rain until dark and then crossed in the rapids so that the Mexicans would not hear the sound of our horses' hooves. We rode four and five abreast. We crossed quickly, and before I knew it we were suddenly among some of Canales's outposts, passing so close to them in the darkness that when their horses shivered in the rain we heard the animals' brass armor jangling and rattling, yet the enemy had no idea of our presence; we could as well have been ghosts.

It was Green, I think, not Fisher, who gave the order to attack — we might have been able to ride right on through them undetected and into Mier, to face Ampudia's men — but that was not the plan.

We heard Green roar — I was surprised to hear it come from behind me, and realized I must have ridden out slightly ahead of the expedition — and my first thought was that he had somehow been injured. He sounded like the mother black bear I had seen kept in a wooden cage above the James River, being fed and fattened through the summer and into the autumn by the man who had trapped her, preparing her like a pig for slaughter.

Rifles and cannons began to go off all around me, and then the woods filled with flashes of light and the odor of burnt powder, and of fresh-cut sap from the limbs and branches torn loose in the sudden fusillade.

Bullets flew all around us, and leaves fell and floated among us, and the horses were barely manageable. In shuttered glimpses we saw the enemy wheeling and galloping south, as Fisher predicted they would.

Shouting and whooping and reloading and firing again, we pursued Canales's men, and in the rout, I looked around for Shepherd but could not find him. Instead, I saw dozens of my own kind riding past, surging, raucous and confident and frightened and joyous — and for myself, I felt neither fear nor joy but was carried on the surge. We were a wave that crashed through the woods and into the town of Mier.

3

VICTORY

We fought as if charmed.

The families in the adobe houses fled into the streets, and we used the butts of our rifles to knock out the walls of first one home and then the next. Canales's men, retreating into Mier, caught the brunt of the fire from Ampudia's men, who were stationed in the center of town, and many of them were cut down more quickly by their own than by us.

There were candles and lanterns still burning in the houses we entered, and we could see in the dim light crude Christ-and-crucifix carvings on the walls, tattered Bibles on the mantels, paintings of Christ, and novenas everywhere.

Canales's and Ampudia's men were trying to follow us into the homes, but they were easy to defend. We had only to station a few men by each door to shoot point-blank each soldier, one by one or two by two, as they attempted to storm those small low doorways.

Soon the entrances were stacked high with dead Mexican

soldiers, and as each one fell his gun was wrested from him and tossed down to those of us who sat or lay beneath windows, where we peered up and fired out at Ampudia's men across the street. Occasionally there was a simultaneity between my one shot, among dozens, and the tumbling of a rider. As if his horse, or the rider himself, had suddenly encountered some rope strung chin-high through the darkness. We moved from one adobe to the next, snuffing out the candles and lanterns left burning by the occupants who had fled.

From their snipers' posts in town, Ampudia's men could look down and take note of our methodical advance by the winking-out last glimmers of candlelight: each new adobe growing dark as we advanced into it, eating our way into the town like some beast gnawing into a carcass, or like a bear ripping through honeycomb.

The Mexicans aimed their cannons at the adobe huts, knocking out head-sized holes with each blast, but in truth these only aided us, for they gave us better windows from which to shoot.

There were too many of us to fit in the windows all at once, so we took turns fighting and sleeping. There was much revelry and good-natured bantering going on among us, and a young man from Rosharon, Joseph McCutcheon, would later write, "There is no sight more grand or sublime than the flash of opposing firearms at the hour of midnight. No sound can produce such an idea of grandeur, and engender such intense excitement, as the ringing report of rifles, the hoarse roar of musketry, the awful thunder of artillery, and the encouraging shouts of fellow man, against unlike men, all mingled in din and confusion.

"This night was by far the most exciting Christmas scene that ever I had witnessed!"

It was not until about midway through the night that a kind of heaviness began to descend on me, a melancholia made all the more profound by its absence in those around me — my fellow Texans were jostling one another for space at the windows, arguing about whose turn it was to get to do more shooting — and I was overwhelmed with homesickness, and with the sure and deep knowledge of having made a terribly wrong choice.

The loneliness felt as heavy as a trunk of lead, and I was suddenly nauseated and wanted no more turns at the window, and no more war, though it was far too late for that.

I moved to the back of the adobe house and took refuge beneath an overturned table. I pretended to be busy cleaning and reloading my gun, examining some malfunction. Several times my friends from LaGrange and Bexar offered me their guns or the weaponry of dead Mexicans, but I declined, told them to go ahead without me.

I made my decision to leave that night, or perhaps in the morning, when I might stand a better chance of finding a horse. I could be back across the river in less than a day, and home three or four days after that. The thought that I could be home in four days, farming, helped get me through that dark night, even as the shouts and whoops of my comrades indicated that they were having the best time of their lives.

I felt a new lightness, and I had the curious thought that this could be somewhat like the feeling James Shepherd might have had in finding his own new path, riding now

59

with Fisher as he was. As if all his life he had labored down the wrong path — had in fact been placed upon the wrong one at birth — and had only now found his own true road, just as my own was to return home, and to leave the warring to soldiers.

I don't think I was very frightened. I was simply hungry for home.

I got up from beneath my table and went searching for Shepherd, to tell him of my plan. I did not want him worrying about me, thinking that I might have been lost in the river crossing, or in battle, beneath some rubble of adobe, hundreds of miles from home.

I found him four houses ahead, in the farthest dwelling of our advance. He was easy to recognize in cannon-fire silhouette, with his missing shoulder. He was leaning against a portal, a long-barreled pistol in his hand. He was not firing it but was instead only staring out the portal. The pistol hung limp from his hand, as if fastened by a thong or bracelet, and he seemed relaxed, though his gaze into the darkness was intent, and he seemed to be doing some sort of mental calculation.

"Does it hurt?" I asked. He seemed to be favoring his wound, trying to lean against the adobe in a way to avoid putting pressure on the other side of his body.

"It always hurts," he said. He glanced at me, then resumed his watching through the cannon-shot portal. "Step behind me — they don't know this hole is here yet. If I shoot, they'll start shooting here, too. I'm just watching, right now. I want to wait until I can get a whole bunch of them."

"Where's Captain Fisher?" I asked. "Where's Green?" He answered with a quick gesture of his head toward a back room. In the pulses of muzzle blast I could see through the open doorway the figures of two men seated at a table, deep in argumentative discussion, sipping soup from small clay bowls. I could smell the soup; it must have been simmering on the stove when they came through this wall. It smelled of chicken stock, with hot peppers and onions, and I realized how famished I was.

I saw now that there was an empty bowl beside Shepherd, and I started to ask if I could have some soup but then did not. Shepherd kept looking at his window keenly, counting and watching.

"Captain says our rifles are better," he said. He glanced down at his pistol. "Their old flintlocks aren't worth shit in this rain. They keep misfiring. They've charged us three times, and we've put them down every time. I'll bet there's a thousand dead Mexicans out there."

Another cannon burst sounded from across the village, and almost instantaneously there was an explosion above our heads, followed by a crumbling slide of adobe shell. A sifting, whispering powder poured down on us, the adobe returning to the sand and clay from which it had come.

Shepherd cursed and drew the big overcoat more tightly around him. I expected him to answer the cannon's fire with fire of his own, but instead his eyes only narrowed and he marked that cannon's position, too, keeping his own unannounced and lethal.

He turned to look at me almost as if surprised that I was still there. I was just about to let him know of my plans, and to ask if there were any messages he wanted me to convey to his family, when something in his demeanor stopped me.

I think he could see that I was done, that I had no heart

or desire to kill any more of the enemy, and there was pity and scorn in his look, and even anger.

Why, you sonofabitch, I thought, with a flash of fire I had not even felt yet for the enemy. *In friendship and loyalty, I have avoided judging you, and now you're daring to judge me.*

"Is there something you wanted to tell the captains?" he asked. He glanced in the direction from which I had come. "Are the other posts secure?"

I looked down at the empty bowl beside his portal.

I was just about ready to say to hell with it: the war, and all my old loyalties to this neighbor, this childhood friend. Sure, Sinnickson had saved his life, but the life of the child I had known was as gone as if the enemy had already claimed him back in Laredo.

I stared at him a moment longer, preparing to leave and to start my own new life, when Ampudia's and Canales's men sounded their fourth charge, sending two whole battalions. Fisher's cunning in keeping the precise extent of our southern advance secret had had an unintended consequence, for now the Mexicans were storming over the top of our farthest adobe, believing it to be unoccupied.

We were obligated to cut them down.

At Shepherd's command, a great number of men whom I had not earlier seen in our adobe came rushing forward, gripping a rifle and a pistol in each hand, and they filled every available crack and crevice in our structure. Someone jammed a rifle into my hands but then shoved me aside, and once more I found myself crouched at an open window, firing into the glimmering, sporadic lightning-light of the war, with the staccato images of the surprised Mexican soldiers throwing their arms skyward as they were shredded by our fusillade, suddenly lifting their arms as if to fly.

We cut them all down, the entire first wave and much of the second; but as we were reloading, the third and then the fourth wave was still coming, slowed only by their stumbling in the darkness over the mountains of their own dead. We could smell the odor of our gunpowder and the dust of crushed and shattered adobe all around us — but there was also another odor, the scent of gallons of blood — and then the Mexicans were at our walls, trying to press themselves through the doors and windows, so that we were having to beat them back with swords and the butts of our pistols and rifles. Ewen Cameron had gone out into an enclosed courtyard and was tearing loose the cobbles from a stone wall, passing them into the house for us to use as weapons in the hand-to-hand fighting.

And though it seemed like ten minutes that we fought in this manner, buying time for our own second wave to reload, it was probably no more than thirty seconds before a hundred of our rifles were answering again, and then a hundred more; and once again, the Mexicans sounded a retreat. Our position was unassailable.

In the silence following their retreat, there was at first only the sound of the injured and the dying, groaning and calling out for help, in the streets of Mier as well as within our own ranks, and the whinnying of injured horses.

We heard a new sound, then, coming from the buildings across the street — a sound like a rushing creek coming from the waterspouts that lined the buildings of commerce.

As the rain had stopped, we did not think it was the sound of runoff and feared instead that it might be coal oil — that they were planning to try to smoke or burn us out.

It was almost first light. In the recovery period for the opposing armies, the regrouping and strategizing, we listened to that newer rushing water sound, and as the gray light of day revealed to us the carnage, we saw, beyond the hundreds of dead Mexicans and the scores of dead horses, that the waterspouts were running red with the blood of all the snipers we had killed atop those buildings. The red rivers of their passing were pouring out onto the cobblestones of the street, and the village dogs, gaunt as skeletons, were tottering among the dead and dying, lapping at the pools and puddles of blood between the cobblestones and drinking straight from the fountain of the drain spouts, their muzzles and whiskers red-splashed.

Now a lone upright, uninjured soldier appeared in the plaza, walking toward us and waving a white flag of surrender, and several among Fisher's command, still drunk on the orgy of blood lust, were keen to cut him down as he approached.

Even as Fisher was ordering them to wait, half a hundred rifles were being cocked, heated barrels bristling from almost every opening, and it was only as the soldier drew nearer that we recognized him as old Ezekiel Smith, who had been captured and made to dress in one of the Mexican uniforms — and the message old Smith carried was not a surrender by the Mexican army nor the town of Mier, but rather a request by Ampudia that *we* surrender.

Green, Fisher, and Cameron, and a few others conferred, and Ezekiel Smith advised, "Do what you want, boys, but they've still got seven hundred or more at the ready, and have sent messengers out to Santa Anna and Huerta and Woll. I believe in another day or two they may have another two or three thousand here."

He stood waiting for our decision, and now Green's and Fisher's voices rose in argument, and in reversal — Fisher counseling surrender in order to be able to fight another day, while Green, Cameron, Wallace, and others wanted to stay and fight at least one more day.

I looked over at Shepherd, who was still standing by that same slotted window. He had tossed the near-useless pistol aside and held a Texan rifle upright, with the hammer already cocked. He was listening to Fisher, but his silent attitude, the righteous indignation and aggression, indicated that he wanted to stay with Green, and to try to kill, with our remaining hundred and fifty or so, the last seven hundred of the enemy before the reinforcements arrived.

And then what? I wanted to shout.

He looked like a monster, without that arm and shoulder, wrapped in that big oilcloth coat. He looked like a gigantic vulture. I had plenty left to live for and was all for surrendering with Fisher, beginning the first steps of gaining my life back, if it could still be had — but our sentiments were divided, and we all grumbled and groused and argued while old Smith waited patiently. If we chose to fight, he would stay; if we surrendered, he would take that message back across the street.

Capitalizing immediately on our indecision, two Mexican officers came hurrying across the street with their own white flags, ostensibly to begin discussing the terms of surrender, but also to assess the morale and injuries among us. As they prattled on with their offers, guaranteeing that we would be treated as prisoners of war, they kept peering into our ranks, taking note.

There was a new flurry of hope and ambiguity among us at the news that if we surrendered we would be treated as prisoners of war rather than as the plunderers and marauders we were. All through the chain of fractured adobe homes, the translation was passed along: *They say they will let us live.* We had slain more than thirteen hundred of their men in an evening, and they said they would let us live.

Fisher and Green continued to argue, more vehemently now, and in the new light I could see that Fisher's thumb was completely torn off.

As they argued, it appeared that Green was beginning to sway Fisher into staying and fighting for at least another day.

But several men had pushed past Fisher, surrendering even before any terms had been agreed on; and as that first flow broke ranks, others followed them. Shepherd, Franklin, and Simmons tried to stop them, as did Cameron and Wallace, but they dodged and twisted past them like fish through a rend in a net. Realizing that with this depletion, further resistance would be futile, thumbless Fisher changed his mind and decided once more to surrender, though he had to hurry after the others to do so, catching up with them only after they had already been escorted into General Ampudia's command.

And suddenly, despite my best intentions to depart and wash my hands of the entire expedition, I found myself victim once again of my own inaction, my tendency to sit and wait and observe rather than to act impulsively. I was now one of two dozen soldiers remaining — Green, Cameron, and

Wallace among us — holed up in the adobe, our numbers whittled suddenly down to less than a tenth of what they had been when we'd departed LaGrange back in the autumn, so full of verve.

We watched Fisher and a few of his stragglers being bound and carted off — the officers with their flags of surrender, as well as old Ezekiel Smith, had disappeared — how much of my own choice was loyalty and how much simple indecision? — and we set about gathering and loading all of the weapons we could find, knowing that we were going to die but preparing, as soldiers and warriors have, across the millennia, to sell our lives dearly.

Such accounting had worked at the Alamo — had yielded the victory a month later at San Jacinto and the birth of a new nation — and even if it had not made sense, it was the only value left to us, it seemed, so we began settling ourselves into the repetition of that story, that cycle. And among those of us who were left, it seemed to me that I was the only one who was now frightened of dying, that the others were accepting it matter-of-factly — the end of this glorious life — as might animals in a stockyard, being prepared for market.

If these men were pondering the things I was pondering as we waited for the day to unfold, they gave no indication of remorse. Instead, there was only grim resolve, filtered with a kind of firm peace or satisfaction, if not quite contentment, and I marveled at this manifestation of pure courage, and at how far I had to travel yet to reach it myself.

For about half an hour we conversed among ourselves, roundly denouncing Fisher and what was perceived to be his cowardice. At any time, Ampudia and Canales could have stormed us, could have peeled loose a couple hundred men and overwhelmed us, but the Mexicans chose instead to wait, chose not to spend any more of their lives or resources in that ten-to-one barter that we had inflicted so far. Green cursed violently and then spat and announced, "Boys, I think we are going to have to cross over."

He looked over at me for a second, then shook his head — *it was Fisher's fault; if only Fisher had remained, we might have been able to make a stand* — and with a sadness I have rarely seen in a man, Green nodded to Simmons to prepare and then hoist a white flag; and as it was lifted, the throng of the Mexican army gave a great cheer of victory and came hurrying across the street to "capture" us.

Before they reached us, Green, rather than allowing our captors to take his rifle from him, began smashing it to pieces with one of the same bloodstained cobbles he had used earlier in the night to crush the head of a Mexican soldier.

Bigfoot Wallace said nothing, though his eyes filled with water. Later in his journal, he would write of the incident: "Never shall I forget the humiliation of my feelings when we were stripped of all our arms and equipment, and led off ignominiously by a guard of swarthy, bandy-legged, contemptible greasers. Delivered over to the tender mercies of these pumpkin-colored Philistines, I could have cried, if I hadn't been so mad."

Even then, not everyone crossed over with us. Whitfield Chalk and Caleb St. Clair, both ministers, had been among those most fiercely committed to standing their ground and fighting — due perhaps to previous arrangements they believed they had made with their Maker — and as the Mexicans hurried across the street to take charge of our surrender, tripping and stumbling over the bodies of their own fallen, Chalk and St. Clair climbed into one of the giant baking ovens in the home in which we were hiding. They would make it out alive, I was to find out much later, waiting until nightfall before slipping out of town and crossing the river, making it all the way back to Texas, where they told President Sam Houston of the heroic events at Ciudad Mier, and of the brave manner in which they had fought their way free of the besiegement.

This was nearly fifty years ago. Once I was able to finally make it back home, for the next five decades I planted crops, season after season, and harvested them, year after year, with very little if anything changing in my fields, even as the world around me changed, or seemed to change.

All wars, like all crops, are the same in that the secret story housed within each seed is undeniable, and that they will always play themselves out in the same manner, again and again, season after season. That belief — that knowledge — is both a terror and an assurance. Terrible, because the content of that seed lies within the hearts of all men, and yet assuring, too, in that we can do little if anything to change it.

They kept us under house arrest for a week while we buried the dead, ours and theirs. Woll and Santa Anna never appeared — perhaps having been informed it was no longer necessary, or perhaps they had never been coming in the first place — and some of Ampudia's and Canales's men guarded us as we worked, while others helped us with the burials.

We carried the dead Texans in carts and on our shoulders

69

to a field outside of town, where we carved their names on hastily lashed crosses, prefacing their last names with only one initial to save time; and we buried the Mexican soldiers in a field at the top of a bluff at the other end of town, laying them down in precise and geometric military fashion.

The digging was easy in the soft sand, and the cold weather was in our favor, as was the dampness of the earth. We were each responsible for burying sixteen soldiers a day — a soldier every hour — and by the middle of the third day we had the task completed, nearly fifteen hundred men buried.

As we worked side by side with our captors and our enemies, a rapport soon developed; and while I would certainly never call it friendship or even affection, there was a kind of respect and peacefulness that accrued as the residue of those labors; and we all took pride, at the end of each day, in the comfort of a difficult job done well.

Early into our work, General Ampudia himself had ridden among us, observing not just the progress of our labors but the features of the men we were burying, as if to memorize them for the inevitable day when their families and loved ones asked for an accounting. He carried a small ledger in his saddlebags, in which he occasionally entered a few phrases and what looked like brief sketches of the men.

General Ampudia had also taken note of the singular sight of Shepherd struggling to excavate his share of the graves — able to plunge the shovel into the loose soil with one hand, but having great difficulty then in lifting the sand out. The deeper Shepherd got, the more sand slid back off his shovel and down the hills of sand surrounding him, so that at times it seemed he was attempting to bury himself rather than any of the fallen enemy. By early afternoon of that first day, Ampudia had ordered one of his lieutenants to give Shepherd a hand up out of his hole, stating that he was a man of mercy and that since clearly we Texans had corrupted a young boy who was not yet old enough to make decisions on his own, he was going to take the boy under his wing.

Fisher protested, climbing out of his hole and laying a hand on Shepherd's arm to detain him. But Shepherd only stared back at him — looking at him as if not recognizing him — and after a moment Shepherd pulled his arm away, and Ampudia laughed, and ordered one of his soldiers to dismount and give Shepherd his horse, while Ampudia walked. The soldier did as he was ordered, knelt and clasped his hands together to form a lower stirrup, and helped lift Shepherd onto his new horse. The next time we saw him, Shepherd was cleaned and scrubbed and wearing a Mexican uniform, and he neither looked our way nor avoided us but moved among and past us as if so completely in another world that the rest of us might never have existed for him: as complete an absence in his past now as was even his arm itself.

We had heard from other veterans that with such injuries there were ghost pains that persisted for decades. But if Shepherd ever felt such pain, he gave no sign of it. He appeared not even to acknowledge the arm's absence, and this gave him a sad kind of grace; and as he moved among us, inspecting our work but never commenting, it seemed that he had buried us, also.

*   *   *

After the burials were completed we began cleaning the streets, scrubbing the blood from the cobblestones. We heated water and lye in iron kettles and cauldrons and scrubbed the stones with fistfuls of river sand until our hands were bleeding. We crawled across the cobbles on our knuckles and knees in the drenching rain that helped wash away the old blood as we scrubbed it free, as well as our own blood.

I have never been colder in my life. We scrubbed until our hands were so numb and torn and wrinkled that we could feel neither the heat nor the lye. As we hauled our iron buckets down the street, steam rose not just from the cauldrons themselves but from our bodies, our sagging, wet clothes draped over us to retain the dwindling heat of our animal bodies, and from the cleansed streets themselves.

Men were hacking and coughing, shivering and chattering. In this endeavor, the Mexican soldiers offered no aid but instead stood guard on the sidewalks, smoking and watching and visiting among themselves, and spelling one another frequently to go warm themselves by the fires within their temporary quarters.

The villagers watched us, too, as did the returning runaway horses, brush-whipped and hungry, saddles sagging sideways from where their cinches had loosened, mouths bloody from where they'd been stepping on their bridles, jerking their heads downward and rattling their teeth. The soldiers led these mounts, Mexican and Texan, into their corrals, and the more feeble among us, the hackers and wheezers, the tubercular rattlers, were assigned the less arduous job of cleaning and currying the remuda for our nearing departure.

We watched for Shepherd, hoping he might be able to inform us of what the Mexicans had in mind for us, and able to intervene somehow on our behalf — but we never saw him, or Ampudia either, and we wondered whether Shepherd had been sent back home.

The rain broke at the end of that fourth day, just as we were finishing cleaning the streets, with a brisk north wind pushing the drizzle southward and a blue sky clearing. The streets steamed in the new sunlight like freshly broken earth, though the cooler temperature of the north wind soon chilled the stones to a gleaming, polished stillness, with the last of the wisps of steam rising in tatters past the tile roofs of the adobe houses.

The city looked gilded, in that new gold late-day winter light, and the Mexican soldiers were still finding a few dead snipers here and there, fallen on those roofs, and in cracks and crevices, and behind chimneys. They were lowering them with ropes from the rooftops, the marksmen stiff as crabs now. And with the light so beautiful and the streets so clean, the town no longer looked so much like a ruin of war, but instead as if it had been a stage for a play; even the dead soldiers being lowered from the roofs, spinning slowly at the ends of their ropes, gave the appearance of actors between scenes.

We had thought that when we finished cleaning their streets we would be allowed to return to our prisoners' quarters, where we could strip out of our stinking, sodden clothes and attempt to dry them on string and rope hung in crisscross lattice above the one small stove. But no sooner had we stood, groaning and stretching our crooked backs, than

Canales came striding out and informed us that we were to begin repairing the damage to the adobe walls.

We were to work through the night, Canales told us, and on through the next day, and the next night — working, he said, until we had all the rubble cleared and every fracture patched, working until it was all as good as new, or better. We were to work ceaselessly, he said, and without food or water, save for whatever bits and pieces the townspeople of the wrecked town and the owners of the homes in which we were laboring chose to dispense to us.

There might have been a revolt right then, even though we had no weapons, but we were too exhausted from the full day of kneeling on the cobbles like penitents; and I think also that the incredible gold light that was pouring into the village was lulling our warrior spirits somehow, almost as if transforming us from rebels and revolutionaries back into the simple yeomen we had once been.

We looked instinctively to our leaders, or to the men who had once been our leaders — the hateful Fisher, with his thumb blown off, and the cocksure, swaggering Green, as well as big Cameron and big Wallace — and when we saw their shoulders slump and saw Green and Fisher turn and begin surveying the damage, we knew that it was possible some of us would end up working ourselves to death, which was certainly not the way we had envisioned achieving our glory when we had first set out: death by washerwoman scrubbing, death by adobe digging.

We began by clearing out the old rubble, forming an assembly line and passing out fragment after fragment, like a bucket brigade — Texans, Mexican soldiers, and townpeople alike. Night had fallen and a low full moon was rising, dropping the temperature precipitously, freezing the wet cobblestones with a glistening skin of ice. We made bonfires of the ruined rafters and chairs and tables, fires so large that they cast heat upon us even from a great distance, the glimmering of the flames reflecting in each icy cobblestone and in the dark eyes of the villagers and the soldiers; and as we worked in that unbroken chain, there was again a strange solidarity that began to be knit among us, captors and captives and townspeople alike.

By morning, we had each of the residences cleaned out completely, and, wobbling with fatigue, dug new pits in which we formed the adobe mixture. Our grimy rags of clothes were crusted with our own blood and the grit of the adobe mixture, and some of the townspeople had found coats for us to wear, and crude gloves.

We worked as we could, sometimes pausing to lie down in the street or next to the adobe pit to pass into a brief unconsciousness of sleep for two or three glorious minutes, before rousing to rejoin our fellow laborers.

The boy who had gotten gangrene in his knee from the cactus needle, Joseph Berry, was working with us, though fading fast. During the battle he had been shot in his good knee as well, so that he was unable to stand without crutches, and we could each smell on him the same telltale odor of rot and loss that had been on Shepherd. But Joseph Berry was even more insistent that he be allowed to keep both legs, regardless of the consequences, and Dr. Sinnickson, beaten down by our travails, did not have the energy to argue with him much. Neither was Captain Green or Fisher inclined to order the legs' removal, figuring that we were all short for this world anyway.

The odor, however, was horrific, and I had the thought that had he been more comely, like Shepherd, rather than as scraggly and scruffy as he was, the doctor and the officers might have worked harder to save him. As it was, he died on the fifth day — in his last hours, he changed his mind and asked Sinnickson to remove the legs, though by that time he was too far gone and we had begun digging his grave even before he passed. We had him buried by that evening, still more bloody and fevered seed for that contested soil.

It took us all that night and the next day and night to finish — Texans and Mexicans alike, working shoulder to shoulder, past the point of exhaustion; but when we were finished, the rebuilt city sparkled, the still damp stucco gleamed like gold, and the hands of destroyers and avengers had been turned instead into those of creators.

We accomplished more in those last two days than we had all autumn, and a greater solidarity had grown between us, captives and captors, for when men have worked together in hard physical labor toward a shared and common goal, their differences and even ancient enmities can be bridged in a way like no other.

We left Ciudad Mier on the seventh day following our surrender, marching in a long, filthy line southward, and attended on every side by the horsebound filade of the victors, the successful defenders of their homeland. And in this manner, I suppose, we were getting what we had desired all along — marching ever southward, as if still on some larger mission: one that we had thought we had understood but of which we were now beginning, in our fatigue and humbling defeat, to realize we had no inkling. That there was a larger mission, a destiny fuller and more powerful than even the one of our own imaginings.

4

ESCAPE

THEY KEPT US in a crude cedar-split corral each night, with a cannon guarding the gate, so that should we try a mass escape, they could level us all. We were kept separate from the horses but afforded the same treatment; we had a communal trough from which to water, were made to void along the perimeter of the corral, and were given but one shovel with which to fling the offending spoor as far from the crude corral as possible.

The nights were bitterly cold, the stars harder and fiercer out in the desert than they had been in the soft hills of home. For warmth we had to build a fire in the center of the corral and then scrape away the coals and sleep bunched up together in the warm ashes. Each morning when we awoke, we looked like ghosts.

We arose at daylight, were given a breakfast of boiled beans, and resumed our march, not even bothering to extinguish our cooking fires, for there was little left in that desolate country to burn. All we possessed were the tattered clothes on our backs, and it was difficult to walk in our riding boots. The cobblers' nails began to protrude into our heels, so we cushioned the boots with cactus pads and short grass; when the country permitted it, we marched barefoot, carrying our ragged boots in our arms.

Shepherd rode with General Ampudia, always looking forward at his new countryside, never back.

Canales's infantry and Ampudia's cavalry kept us surrounded constantly, and from somewhere a military band had joined us, sometimes marching silently beside us, carrying their bright, brassy instruments large and small, and other times playing them loudly. We marched on blindly, unmindful of where we were going or of what fate awaited us, pale prisoners in an alien land, advancing across the desert like a gaudy and inept circus.

Whenever we came to a village, our procession halted at the nearest creek and the Mexicans bathed, polished their boots and brass until they shone, and groomed their horses. They slicked back their dark hair and, reassembling in precise military order, proceeded into the village, with the band marching alongside us, blaring. We were paraded around the town square while the villagers cheered.

In each new village there would be bright decorations, as if for a feast, with colorful ribbons and articles of clothing hanging from Maypoles and strung on clotheslines stretched across the streets and between buildings: scarves, rebozos, serapes, dresses, men's sequined pants. Paper banners with the slogans of ETERNAL HONOR AND IMMORTAL AMPUDIA and GLORIA Y GRATITUDE AL BRAVO CANALES were everywhere. Church bells pealed and clanged as we were marched around and around the town square, no longer warriors but objects of derision and entertainment. Children danced among us, shaking gourds and rattles made from bones of indeterminate origin. In Nueva Reynosa, an old Indian ran up to us, flashing a mirror in our faces.

In other villages — perhaps towns that had produced some of the soldiers who had been killed in the battle for Mier — there was no celebrating, but instead we were pelted with stones and rotten eggs and called hard names. We were deprived of food and water in these towns, or given the murkiest, brownest, saltiest water imaginable, so that sometimes my own dreams were no longer of escape but instead of pure, clean water, even a single cup of it. All that I now desired I had once possessed.

We soon realized that despite the rigors of the journey, the forced marches through the countryside were infinitely preferable to staying overnight in the villages. In the desert, the camaraderie between us and our captors usually returned, and we preferred the open air of the wilderness to the humiliations of town.

"While marching," Bigfoot Wallace said, "we can at any rate breathe the pure, fresh air of heaven without being hooted at and reviled by the mob and rabble that always collects around us wherever we halt."

At the feasts that celebrated our captivity we were given only beans, and never quite enough. We had been given old coats to replace the thin tatters in which we'd previously been shrouded — our "uniforms" — and I would try to save a few dry beans each day from the bag that was offered to us for cooking — slipping a fistful of them, dry and rattling, into my coat pocket before the bulk of the bag was poured into the group caldron. On the next day's march I would finger them in my coat pocket, examining each one like a talisman before choosing one to place in my mouth.

I would suck on the hard bean, making it last as long as I could, the bean providing some moisture as I salivated, and, later, when it was finally softened enough to chew, a trace of nourishment, giving enough energy for another ten paces, or another hundred.

We pushed on, southward.

We thought about escape all the time. Bigfoot Wallace and Ewen Cameron thought about it most insistently.

Although the officers realized that Wallace was an excellent soldier, they did not know of his fame among the Texas Rangers. They were familiar with Cameron, however. Back when Canales had been a mercenary in the Texas Revolution, fighting on our side for a while, Canales and Cameron had fought nearly to the death in an argument over which one of them would get to ride a certain horse. It looked for now as if Canales the Decapitator had won that argument, and as he rode alongside Cameron — the Scot, walking, nearly as tall as the horse was at the shoulders — it was evident that Canales found great mirth in the present situation, and just as evident that Cameron was simmering.

Each night in our prison camp inside the corral, Wallace — who more and more was becoming our de facto leader — had to counsel restraint. *Escape* was the unspoken catechism in everyone's mind — it had become our identity, our reason for being — but each night Wallace reminded us to bide our time and to wait for the single best chance, that we would have only one opportunity, and that we would need to be ready, eternally ready, to make the most of it.

Our old captains had all but deserted us. They had ceased their day-and-night squabbling — having nothing left, finally, to argue about — and for the most part kept to themselves down at one end of the corral. Because they were officers, they were afforded more respect by our captors — sometimes, in the evenings, they would even be given a cigar to smoke. Green still occasionally made an effort to stay connected to his former command, and while Fisher was interested only in his own survival, the fires of escape and revolution still burned bright in Green's eyes, or so it seemed at night, when he would come over to our low fire to visit. He would sit next to Wallace and appeared to mind neither the unspoken weakening of his own rank nor the unofficial rise of Wallace's. He seemed like one of us, just a man who had made a poor choice.

In the daytime, however, Green drifted back into conversation with Fisher, and then the two men and their different desires were combined once more, incompatible but as inseparable as they had been at the beginning of the journey. Sometimes, believing it unfit for officers of any kind to be made to march so far, Canales and Ampudia would allow Fisher and Green to ride with them — though always Ampudia kept Fisher separated from Shepherd, whose black hair was getting longer, and whose already olive skin was growing even darker.

And in the daytime, trudging through my comrades' dust, dreaming of water, I would grip the fistful of beans in my coat pocket, would examine each one in my hand, rolling them between my fingers like pebbles. I would think of the incredible power latent in each seed — of the way a single bean, unfolding from beneath the soil, could shove aside a stone; and of the way a handful of such seeds could transform a barren land into a crop of bounty — and such dreams, such images, gave me strength, without my yet having to put a single bean into my mouth, even as other men around me were stumbling, falling to their knees.

Sometimes when this happened a soldier would circle back around on his horse and dismount and offer a hand to the fallen captive to help him back to his feet, offering him a sip of water from his canteen; though other times, the circling-back captor would instead give the supplicant a lashing across his neck and back. Gradually we came to understand dimly that our captors' wrath was most likely to be highest when the distances between one village and the next were greatest, and we tried to adjust our collapses accordingly. We helped each other along as we could, and tried to maintain a steady pace.

So festive was the celebration of our arrival in Matamoros that we stayed for two nights rather than one, and Green and Fisher were allowed a new set of clothes and were boarded in a lieutenant's home, and I began to understand that the more powerful our leaders could be made to appear, the greater the cause for celebration, and the greater the reflected glory cast upon the conquerors.

The extra night's rest, even though we were housed in a cow pen, was blissful. Three more of our number had died from consumption — we had stopped and buried them along the trail — and had we not gotten the extra night's rest in Matamoros, I believe that we would have lost a dozen more.

Among us, only Wallace and Cameron seemed impervious to fatigue and unable to acknowledge defeat.

In the evenings I played cards with boys like Orlando Phelps and Billy Walker. We played not in the reckless style of young men but cautiously now, like old men; though our greatest bluff was the game itself, and the casual pretense that all those among us who played would still be with us at journey's end. That our path would somehow lead us back home — or anywhere else, for that matter, other than the abyss.

In Monterrey, our officers stayed once again in a private home. We were in the city for a week and never saw them once during that entire time. It was almost too much for men like Cameron and Wallace to bear, but our jealousy and resentment were tempered by the valuable recuperation time we were gathering.

Captains Green and Fisher boarded in a colonel's house on a bluff overlooking the city. They had been outfitted in more new clothes, grander than ever, which they now wore on the march ever south. And without meaning to gloat — indeed, expressing marvel and amazement at their fortune, rather than triumph — they allowed how they had been entertained on both the piano and the guitar by the colonel's daughters, whom they had found, in Captain Green's words, "attractive and compelling, altogether satisfactory."

They had danced and gone to lavish dinners every evening, being entertained by the city's elite, who were curious and anxious to witness firsthand this sampling of the barbaric Texas rebels they had been hearing about. Captain Green described the Mexican women he encountered during this strange week as "winged creatures" and said that they danced "with a bewitching, ethereal, gossamer touch."

They discovered we were bound for the prison at Hacienda del Salado. Green and Fisher said that some of the women with whom they had danced had blanched on hearing that it was our destination and had informed them that it was one of the worst prisons in Mexico, one from which few ever exited alive. It was finally this knowledge more than anything else that emboldened us to make our first attempt at escape.

In the evenings, as we talked about our escape a consensus began to develop, which was that it would be best to make our break from a town or village rather than out in the middle of the desert. A town or village, while possibly offering more resistance, might also yield more loot.

But we still argued when would be the best time to make our rush. Many believed that it should be under cover of darkness, though Bigfoot Wallace, crafty as ever, postulated that morning might be best. He had noticed that the Mexican soldiers each slept with their firearms, but that at breakfast they stacked them in a neat pile while they stood in line to get their grub. He had noted also that the Mexican officers, who were allowed to dine first, had been in the habit recently of going off into the countryside shortly after breakfast for a morning ride with Green and Fisher.

Wallace and Cameron told us to be ever vigilant, particularly in the mornings, that we would recognize the moment when it arrived, that we would know in an instant that it was our time to rise.

We could each feel it building. Our guards seemed jumpy

and were quieter than usual. And with this new tension, this new silence, there were now those among us who were beginning to falter at the thought.

Wallace had an eye for these falterers and spent time with each of them, counseling that they would be better off participating in the escape, for if we failed, we all failed together, but if Wallace and Cameron and their followers succeeded, the wrath of the Mexican army would be visited upon those who remained.

Old Archibald Fitzgerald, a veteran of the Napoleonic Wars, who had signed up as much out of boredom as patriotism, was ambivalent, hoping that his status as a British citizen might gain him some kinder treatment, or even release. Another prisoner, Richard Brenham, was far more upset — inconsolable, truthfully. He confided to anyone who would listen that he had been haunted lately by an inescapable premonition that his career was "shortly to be closed," and had even been hinting at suicide, he said, for "release from this painful thralldom."

The first day out of Monterrey, en route to the next village, Saltillo, Cameron approached us one by one and told us to be ready. We languished for weeks in Saltillo, however, without an opportunity — and growing weaker — and then were marched farther south, to Hacienda del Salado, where Cameron told us that this time we had to escape, or die, and that we would make our attempt the next morning.

Only Charles Reese was solidly against the escape plan. He pointed out that we were now more than three hundred miles from home, an observation that infuriated Cameron. Reese shook his head and argued further. "Even if you manage to escape into the countryside, the local militias will cut you down."

It was his use of the word *you* rather than *us* that made me think afterward that he was the one who tipped off the officer directly in charge of guarding us — Colonel Barragan. The next morning, with all of us waiting anxiously for some sign from Cameron, we were surprised to see that Barragan checked in on us an hour earlier than usual. He seemed extraordinarily suspicious, and some accused Reese outright of having alerted him. The more charitable among us — of whom I was not one — believed that Reese had escape plans of his own and was concerned that our attempt might jeopardize them.

Regardless, the plan was foiled that day, and later that night Cameron urged Reese once more to change his mind, warning him that the break would need to be made very soon, maybe even the next day, and even if he had to make it "all alone and single-handed."

Reese remained unconvinced. "You have sinned away your days of grace," he told us that night, staring into the fire and speaking calmly. "What was courage and wisdom on one side of the border would be madness and weakness on this side. There is only this one earthly life," Reese said. "Regardless of your beliefs in a hereafter, or a merciful God, we are flesh but once, and our choices must be made wisely."

Bigfoot Wallace was listening, pensive for once, but Cameron cursed and rose from the fire and stalked away.

Our sleep was fitful, and my fishing acquaintances and I visited late into the night, speaking not so much of war or freedom but about the homes we had left behind.

Jimmy Pinn spoke of the berry cobbler that his mother

made each Sunday in the spring, and Curtis Haieber told of going turkey hunting with his father.

"I even miss the work," I told them, "digging stumps, hauling stones out of the field, plowing, cutting stovewood. It wasn't any more tiring than this, and you felt better at the end of the day."

In that younger life, there had been a security, even sanctity, in the regular cycles and rhythms, even if harsh. And were not these things — bygone, now — every bit as much the essence of freedom as our current campaign for contested, distant territories?

We were still just children. We talked into the night about all the things that were most precious to us, and, I think, without ever speaking directly about it, we formed the necessary courage that would be required in the morning — to take on our armed captors barehanded, and to be prepared to fight, again, to the death.

Since Monterrey we had been receiving rice for breakfast, lunch, and dinner, which was a wonderful improvement over beans. I still carried a dusty fistful of dried beans in my coat pocket as an emergency ration, but now that we had new stores of rice, our spirits were better, and we were no longer beset by the diarrhea that had begun to plague us. Occasionally, as they had with the beans, our captors threw in a few scraps of meat: hoofs, gristle, ears, tongues, internal organs. Any offal they did not want was ours. A dead snake encountered in the middle of the trail. The shell of an armadillo. A vulture that one of their marksmen shot from the sky, the great black bird plummeting from such a height that it exploded upon impact, leaving only a smeared mess, and feathers.

That next morning, Colonel Barragan checked in on us early again before heading into the hills for his morning ride with Green, Fisher, Canales, and Ampudia, as well as Shepherd, who continued to ride with Ampudia. We kept spooning rice from our gourds, watching the officers' cavalry grow more distant, and when they were tiny specks, Ewen Cameron tossed his hat high into the air where all could see it, and with a wild whoop he charged the two guards at the gate, knocking them both to the ground, and with our own wild roars the storm of us poured through the gate and fell upon our startled captors as they were still eating their own breakfast.

One irregular, John Robson, had made a weapon by wrapping a stone in his coat and swinging it around and around, leveling any soldier who came near him. He spun through the Mexicans like a tornado, with others trailing in his wake, and we were able to get to the cache of rifles just steps ahead of the soldiers.

On the trail, they might have been our benefactors at times, and even, occasionally, our commiserates, but now we fell upon them and mowed them down — swinging stonecoats, firing rifles, and even turning their own cannon upon them. Bigfoot Wallace had seized a bayonet and was fighting hand to hand. There was pain in our captors' faces, but what I remember more were the expressions of surprise and sorrow.

A soldier and a Texan wrestled for a musket, and the musket discharged at such close range that the powder burns ignited the Texan's ragged coat. He ran howling among us and leapt into one of the horses' watering troughs.

More a way station for supplies and a crude military fortress than a true village, Hacienda del Salado was a lonely place, built of stone in the middle of a small barren valley, between the foothills — beyond which stretched the cold blue mountains of the Sierra de la Paila — and as we gained the upper hand, the two hundred or more villagers began abandoning it, fleeing into the surrounding countryside.

We were fighting amid a hail of bullets, and the air was filled with flashing swords and knives and bayonets. Runaway horses were knocking us to the ground, and men were astraddle one another, pounding their brains out with stones and boulders.

In little more than ten minutes we took the fort, and then immediately became divided amongst ourselves. There were those of us who wanted to strike out for home, but there was another faction who wanted to loot and plunder first. The homelanders, as I had come to think of those of us who preferred Green's command, sought to gather the frightened mules and horses, while the renegades roamed the stone fortress, routing those terrified villagers who crouched in hiding, commandeering all they could find of worth in that barren desert city. By the time they were done, they had gathered 160 muskets and carbines, a dozen jeweled swords and as many pistols, and $1,400 worth of silver, as well as three mule-loads of ammo: and once again, we were an army.

There were five dead among our number, and twenty dead Mexicans. Included among our dead were Richard Brenham, who had been tormented days earlier by the premonitions of his death, and the veteran of the Napoleonic Wars, Archibald Fitzgerald: a particular tragedy, we were to find out later, as there had already been a letter en route to Mexico City that stated his release had been secured, as he had been hoping, by the British consul.

Up in the hills, we were to find out later, the cavalry that was escorting Green and Fisher on their morning ride heard all the gun- and cannon-fire and looked down and saw the women and children fleeing Hacienda del Salado, and then the soldiers themselves fleeing — and in their fury, they wanted to return the betrayal by killing Green and Fisher right then and there, and to ride to the defense of the fort.

But Green argued passionately that Colonel Barragan's orders were to transport him and Fisher to Mexico City for trial, and that the order to execute them could not take precedence over these other orders, which had been given by a general. Even Ampudia and Canales relented in the face of that argument, and so after some discussion they left ten of the cavalry up in the hills with Green and Fisher while the remainder rode back down into Hacienda del Salado to join the fray.

We were just leaving when Barragan and his little group rode up and tried to block our exit. Colonel Barragan dismounted and walked up to Ewen Cameron, and with all one hundred and fifty Texas muskets aimed at him, Barragan ordered Cameron to surrender.

Cameron laughed and declined — we all began to laugh — and with that, he pushed past Barragan, as did Bigfoot Wallace, walking stride for stride next to him, and the rest of us followed, with our ragged assemblage of booty, some of us on horseback and others walking or leading pack mules burdened with silver or ammunition.

We forgot to take water. We did not think about water. We did not know the countryside.

Colonel Barragan and his men followed us, good soldiers that they were. They remained always at a distance — too far for us to shoot — but always on our tracks.

We took turns walking and trotting and riding the mules and horses, and covered nearly ninety miles in those first twenty-four hours. Only three more days like that, and we would be home. I, for one, believed we were going to make it.

By the end of that first twenty-four hours, we were desperate for water and not a little inconvenienced for food. We had been traveling down the center of the dusty road that led due north — our plan was to pass through La Encarnacíon and then veer west of Monterrey, through the rougher country of Venadito and Boca de los Tres Rios.

Just outside of La Encarnacíon, we decided to approach a home, all hundred and fifty of us, and request food and water. But the windows fairly bristled with guns at our approach. We noted that there were a few horses hitched outside belonging to Mexican soldiers and cavalry, and so we rode around that home. As we rode past, cries and calls went up, *"Soldados desgraciados!"* and though we tried to stay out of their range, they lobbed some distant shots at us anyway, one of which struck a young irregular, Herbert Garner, in the head, felling him instantly.

We did not have time to bury him, and instead trotted on, leaving him behind for Barragan's men, who were still trailing us, to bury. Now there was one more open space available on the back of a horse, though we knew our stock could not keep up the pace we had set for them that first twenty-four hours, that already we had almost ridden them into the ground.

As the pangs of hunger and thirst worked on us we began to squabble and unravel yet again, and rather than simply dividing in two groups, as had been our earlier tendency — one man choosing Green's leadership, and another Fisher's — we began to separate in what seemed like infinite directions, as if our differences were now no longer simply oppositional but as diffuse as gusts of wind.

That afternoon we met an Englishman heading in the opposite direction, riding a tall old gray mule and dressed in a long formal coat, carrying a parasol to protect his balding head from the cold but brilliant winter sun. He hailed us and visited with Cameron and Wallace for some time, informing them that he was traveling the wilderness for his own edification — and when we asked about the route ahead of us, he said that we would do well to stay on the main road all the way to the border — that although we would probably encounter a few soldiers and cavalry, there was none anywhere in such force as to outnumber us.

The Brit seemed delighted by our derring-do, by the valor of our grand escape, and wished us Godspeed, and before riding southward (toward Colonel Barragan's still-trailing little force) he paused and asked if there were any artists among us. To my surprise, one of the boys I had fished with on the Rio Grande, Charles McLaughlin, eased forward on the frothy, leg-trembling mule he was sitting, and raised his hand.

The Brit was delighted, and, still astride his own mule,

nudged his animal forward and made a great show of presenting to Charles McLaughlin a blank journal and a little leather-bound satchel containing pens of varying gauges, and little vials of ink, as well as some chalk and pastels.

"You are on the grand adventure of your life," he said. "You must record it, not for posterity, but for yourself." A lone cloud was drifting across the sky, and as it passed now before the sun, the Englishman folded his parasol and, before placing it in an empty rifle scabbard attached to his saddle, reached out with it and touched Charles McLaughlin on the shoulder as if knighting him. He turned toward Wallace and Cameron then, studying them as if evaluating them for a painting — and then the cloud was past, exposing his bright pate to the sun's cold brilliance again, and he pulled the parasol from his scabbard and hoisted it once more and then rode on.

We found our first and last water at Agua Nieta. The spring was alkaline, surrounded by calceous stone walls of great antiquity, erected to keep animals out; but we knocked out the walls and gate and drove our remuda right into the warm shallow spring, where we slid down from our saddles and lay on our bellies like pigs, drinking among the mules and horses as they too wallowed and thrashed in the salty pond. Our thrashings were soon soiling the spring with horse piss and green mule shit, as well as the vomit of soldiers who had drunk too much too fast, and their own piss and shit and grime as they stripped out of their filthy rags and laundered them, standing ankle-deep in the turmoil and scrubbing themselves with gouty fistfuls of the chalky mud.

I and a few others crouched at the edge of the salty pond — the water was lowering before our very eyes — and quickly filled our flasks and canteens, splashed water on our bare faces and arms, and cleaned ourselves as best as we could. We looked backwards often, to see that the waver of Barragan's men was larger, becoming more and more distinct — and finally leaders rousted the wallowers from the now vile spring and told us we needed to be moving again.

Charles McLaughlin was seated on one of the stone walls, sketching the scene before him quickly, and by the time Wallace and Cameron had the men and their stock rounded up, he had finished his sketch. Those of us who cared to look at it agreed that it was almost realistic, but we were a bit surprised that it had come from his hand, and from his eye.

He had made the scene appear almost idyllic, with very little of the squalor.

In that regard, the picture was false, but in the sense that it presented ourselves the way we would have liked to be seen, it was true.

Briefly strengthened, the wallowers began to argue with Cameron about his decision to stay on the road. "Let's go up into the mountains," they said. "The cavalry can never find or follow us there." And I regret to say that although I had heretofore been in complete agreement with everything Cameron and particularly Wallace had counseled, in this instance I was among those clamoring to go up into the mountains and perhaps cross back over into Texas, farther west, through the Sierra Madres.

Only Cameron and Wallace wanted to stick to the main

road. But now that the war was breaking up, their power was fading, and the hundred-other of us had our way.

What did we know of mountains? Only enough to be dangerous to ourselves. When we looked back, we rejoiced, at first, on seeing that Barragan's men had paused at the foot of the mountains, watching our ascent, and had not followed. Indeed, some of them turned back, and from our initial vantage, already some thousand feet above them, we had cheered. Others of Barragan's men watched us a while longer and then rode on farther north: and to a man, we felt that our choice had been the right one.

Barragan's men had not long been gone from sight before we began to encounter our first difficulties. What had seemingly offered us salvation, the mountains' ruggedness, was also what threatened to break us, for the pitch became steeper and our footing less certain in the scree at the base of the cliffs we sought to scale. Having never ridden horses in the mountains, we had not realized there might be terrain too steep for them or even the mules, and soon we were having to lead them up and over the larger boulders and through the scree, horses and men sliding and scrambling alike. We were having to pull and push them up through slots and chimneys, our work made all the more impossible by the heavy burdens of our looting.

Some of the clastic rocks were still sharp-edged, remnants from a long-ago exploded earth — and the razor edges of those shattered rocks slashed our tattered boots and shoes and sliced the fetlocks of our pack train, so that we left behind us a wandering ribbon of red, like a skein of bright thread laid down on a map.

There was no water, only brush and cactus and shattered stones. The vertical walls of granite were flecked with dark fragments of mineral so shiny that, when climbing with our faces pressed tight against those cliffs, we could sometimes see our own eyes reflected as if in blackened mirrors. It was an unsettling image — as if we had somehow been captured by the mountain and were now moving around inside it, or as if we were looking across time and space to another version of ourselves.

We kept ascending, a diminished army of thieves and gentlemen, but by nightfall had made only a few more hundred feet. We made camp on a narrow ledge, roping ourselves to crags and pinnacles, and slept fitfully in the freezing wind. All night, whenever I drifted off for even a few minutes of slumber, I dreamt of falling, as apparently did many of the rest of the men, and all night the mountain rang with our sleepy shouts of fear, while our unhobbled horses and mules wandered off to search in vain for a blade of grass, of which there were none, only stone and creosote bushes.

In the harsh cold red light of morning we awakened and understood, each of us, that the horses and mules would have to be slaughtered.

We set about this task methodically, using our knives and jeweled swords. It was sloppy, inefficient work, and as the floundering mules and horses staggered about bleeding to death, we raced after them, laboring to hold our empty gourds beneath leaping gouts of blood; and when the gourds were filled, we drank directly from the animals' necks, gorging once more, while the rocks beneath us, like our faces and bodies, became painted bright crimson in the morning sun. The giants, Cameron and Wallace, were of invaluable assistance in this gruesome task, and worked with grim word-lessness, as if we had entered another land where language no longer mattered.

Charles McLaughlin followed us, sketching it all.

After we had drunk the blood of the horses and mules, we began carving on them; and because there was no wood for making real cooking fires, we set fire to the creosote bushes, a hundred or more such little fires burning all around us, and we cooked the meat as best as we could in that manner, searing it to warm gray on sticks held over the oily black smoke of the smoldering creosote.

Many of our shoes and boots had fallen apart completely on the rocks below, so we cut up the horses' saddles, and the bloody hides themselves, in crude attempts to make sandals. And yet, we were not despairing. High up on the mountain, it seemed to us that we were free, even in our misery. We divided our $1,400 of silver, giving each man his share.

We pushed on higher up the mountain. At the next crest we paused to look down. Below us, like the spoor of our free-dom, lay hundreds of charred and smoking bushes. The bright shattered rocks seemed almost alive in their brilliance now, and the skinned and shredded carcasses of nearly a hundred mules and horses lay broken open on the rocks.

Curtis Haieber, Jimmy Pinn, and Robert Gosk decided to stop for a while and nurse their feet. The rest of us kept moving, but by morning two more dropped out. Charles Mc-Laughlin paused to sketch the deserters.

We ascended a ridge and were up out of the creosote and chaparral. The walking should have been easier, but it wasn't, and by noon three more men dropped their packs and sat down and waved to the rest of us and told us to go on, go on, *mas alla*, farther on.

That night we couldn't sleep. Our tongues were swollen and beginning to turn black. There was no more discussion of reaching the Rio Grande, or even of leaving this godforsaken country. We desired only water, and the next day we split apart further, with Cameron and Wallace still commanding a core of about fifty men and the rest unbraided into little tribes of five and six, with the agreement that any of us who found water would send up smoke signals.

McLaughlin stayed with us. He had been sketching Wallace and Cameron, drawing them even as they walked, and now he had begun to sketch me, too, which made me feel worthy and officerlike.

I still had the last beans in my pocket: a smaller fistful, but still a fistful. I had lost all hunger, craved only water, and was allowing myself one bean per day, which I sucked on from morning to evening. As we trudged, I counted and examined each bean — I had gone into the mountains with forty — and I wondered how many, if any, would be left when I was finally out of the mountains.

Later in the day, we abandoned our rifles and packs. Even Bigfoot Wallace lay down his musket, building a little cairn around it so that he might one day return to it. He was moving slowly; it took him an hour to perform this small task, and his usually sharp mind was torpid — he appeared befuddled at times by the choice of all the rocks that were available to him — and then we proceeded on, feeling, for a while, almost winged in our lightness.

There was little vegetation of any kind — we gnawed at the black lichen we sometimes found growing on the rocks, so that to anyone watching us from above, it would have seemed that we were gnawing at the rocks themselves — and when we encountered an occasional clump of prickly pear cactus, we dug these up with bleeding hands and chewed greedily at the spiny pads and succulent roots, trying to avoid piercing our swollen black tongues on the cactus spines.

That night we lay collapsed in the high desert. No one spoke, no fires were built, no sentries were posted. It was our fourth day without water. It seemed that all the water in the world was gone.

Overnight, John Alexander, who was sleeping but a short distance away from me, dreamt of water. In the morning, he told us that in his dream he was back at his home in Brazoria County, where there was a great feast in his honor, with friends and family, but he kept pushing all the wonderful food aside.

"I craved water, only water," he said, "and when this was forthcoming I emptied each jar as it was brought to me and then called for more." He shook his head slowly, exhibiting the same torpor that had afflicted Bigfoot Wallace. "Each draught seemed only to inflame my thirst, and yet no one of the vast company present seemed astonished at the amount of water I drank. My thirst was unquenchable."

We all felt a great envy that he had received such offering, even if only in a dream, and I felt a great loneliness, that I had been sleeping near him but had received no such dream, that it had passed over me and chosen him.

And when he, too, split off from our larger group, choosing instead to try to crawl back down off the mountain, no one tried to discourage him, and an older man, an ex-officer from Zachary Taylor's campaign in New Mexico, Major George Oldham, joined him, as did a few others. We watched as they crawled away across the high desert like animals, disappearing over the rim of the mountain, looking like a line of slow-moving bears: disappearing, bound for the salt-desert below.

They found water. Gnawing again at the roots and eating even the thin, salty soil itself, they had continued descending until they stumbled finally onto a waterfall gushing straight out of the mountain.

There was no prefatory seep or spring above it, but simply a great cannonade of water jetting from a port, a rift in the mountains, and splattering onto the rocks below, in which, over the centuries or millennia, the water had carved a wide and deep pool before trailing away back down the mountainside, running as a small creek for a while and then disappearing back into the soil.

It had been running just a thousand feet below us all along.

John Alexander and his group spent the rest of the day lying in that pool, bathing and drinking and eating the last of the now rotten horse meat one of them had stashed in his pack. It was not the feast of his dream of the night before, he told them: it was better.

In the meantime — never dreaming of Alexander's success (neither did we see the smoke from their cooking fires), we staggered north, still clinging to the mountain's spine, unwilling to give up any of our hard-earned vantage. Two more of our number — Buster Toops and O. M. Martin —

drifted off and never returned. They, unlike so many dozens of others, did survive, and upon their return to Texas their accounts were well publicized, recorded into the strange vault of written and remembered history, while the exploits, the failures and successes, of so many others vanished unknown or were never told.

Toops and Martin licked rainwater from little depressions in the scooped shallows of rocks over on the shadier north side of the mountain, when they could find them. They would hike until they collapsed into sleep, then awaken and hike, again for days at a time, before collapsing again, until one day they came upon a feral ox.

Martin, unlike almost all the other men, had retained his musket; he killed the animal, and once again they drank its blood, sucking it straight from the wound. When they had gotten out all that they could in that manner, they used the tiny flint from the musket to gut the ox and were finally able to open it enough to be able to extract and roast the liver and a few other organs.

They came eventually into a little valley, where they encountered a few small, remote ranches. Here they were treated with kindness and hospitality, and with their stolen silver they purchased food and supplies and then veered north and east, back toward Laredo, the site of our original plundering.

They reached the river and floated across on a fallen log, shouting and whooping. Their joyous splashing alerted a few townspeople, who, believing themselves to be under attack again, responded with a volley of gunfire that successfully steered Toops and Martin away from town and back into the brush. But it was native brush, and native soil, and they staggered on with great joy to San Antonio, where their selective tale was received with awe.

John Alexander and Major Oldham's waterfall group had continued on, falling apart in the meantime, dwindling and scattering, lost and dying in the desert until finally only Alexander and Oldham remained. Oldham found a beehive and was mauled by the bees when he tried to scoop the honey out with his bayonet — they followed him on a dead run for two miles before he collapsed, unable to go any farther, and was very nearly stung to death. He was ill for several days — Alexander stayed with him and cared for him — and no sooner had they started moving again than Alexander fell ill, wracked by fever, and Oldham stayed and cared for him.

When they finally reached the Rio Grande, they dismantled an old stock pen, built a pole raft, and floated across in moonlight, back to the freedom of the Republic of Texas, although not yet back to safety.

The village of Laredo had, via Toops and Martin's accounts in San Antonio, received word of the expedition's escape and had posted lookouts. Alexander and Oldham had to skirt the town and hide in the brush to avoid capture by the local militia. It took them another month to reach San Antonio, where they too were received as heroes.

Still others split off from Cameron and Wallace's group. They struck out on their own, descending back into the desert, although they failed to encounter the waterfall that Alexander and Oldham had found.

It was still cool up in the mountains, but out on the desert, the weather had turned warmer. We could see the shimmering heat waves rising from the desert below, and could see where many of the men had tossed their threadbare blankets on top of scrub brush to make crude tents, and then crawled beneath them to die. Others scratched at the thin soil with their fingernails, digging as if searching for buried treasure; but we saw then, as they wallowed in that freshly dug depression, that they were simply trying to use that brief coolness of the newly exposed soil to take some of the radiant heat from their fevered, baking bodies.

They appeared to be eating the cool dirt they had just dug, applying it to their cracked and blistered mouths. They drank their own urine.

There were others strung out all over the mountainside and crawling around in the valleys. The mountain was bleeding men. I don't know why we stayed on top. Cameron and Wallace appeared confused, directionless, almost lifeless. I tried to formulate a plan, tried to dream an idea, a strategy, anything that might give us hope, no matter how improbable, but could think of nothing, could instead only desire, like the others, water. Even a single jar would have been enough, even a single swallow.

Looking back at the trail of our misery, we could see rafts of vultures, looking like columns of black smoke, circling the ruin of horses and mules several miles distant. Anyone could look up at the mountain and see where we had been and where we were going.

Indeed, it turned out, entire villages had been observing the stupor of our progress and our descent. Barragan's men, now well rested, well watered, well armed, had ridden around to the north, knowing that that was where the mountain would spit us out. They were waiting patiently there, at the mouth of the Cañon de San Marcos, where they began snaring Texans one by one and two by two, like fish in a weir.

We who were left remained far atop the mountain, watching the soldiers below, still waiting for us. Our upper group had dwindled from seventy to twenty. We had no water, no food, no weapons, and it was not going to rain; neither did it seem that any divine intervention was going to reach us. Charles McLaughlin had stopped sketching and instead sat numbly, staring, as we all were, at the smoke from the soldiers' fires far below.

There was nothing to do but surrender, no other alternative in the world if we were to have another chance at life, yet Wallace and Cameron seemed unable to discuss this fact, and I saw that it was up to me to broach the subject, that it was my responsibility to try to save myself, as well as the tatter of men scattered around me.

I fingered the beans in my pocket. The men were dying, boiling on the rocks, desiccating like withered salamanders; I was not sure they had the strength to descend, even if they could be persuaded.

"If we are to have any hope of fighting again," I said, "we must survive." My voice was a croak, and I could see now that many of the men did not even understand what I was talking about; that although they had seen the activity below and witnessed the smoke rising from the soldiers' cooking fires, their minds were no longer making even the simplest of connections. Issues such as freedom or captivity no longer existed for them. There was just one thing in the world: the next rattling breath, followed by another, followed by another.

Cameron bowed his chin to his chest, then shook his head slowly. Wallace reached over and put a hand on his shoulder, then rose and went around to each of the fallen men, touching them lightly, and one by one, we rose, all except Cameron, and proceeded down the mountain, limping and wobbling, toward the smoke. When I paused to look back, I saw that Cameron had finally risen and was following, and although he was bullheaded and often violent beyond reason, I felt a wave of guilt at being responsible, even partially, for the surrender of so uncompromising a man.

Skeletons already, we stumbled down the mountain, falling often and helping each other up, making our way toward the distant threads of smoke. When we arrived in the camp and saw the too familiar sight of our comrades housed once again in makeshift corrals, we were rewarded for our surrender with a few sips of water. Colonel Barragan escorted Wallace and Cameron away from the rest of the skeletons and placed them in their own separate corral.

From time to time we would look across at them, peering through our rails to where the two big men sat hunch-shouldered and conversing, and as we recovered and felt the flow of life returning to us, many of the men allowed that they felt awful and lamented that they had not stayed on the main road all the way home, as the Englishman had advised.

For the next few days, Barragan's cavalry scoured the countryside, bringing in stragglers. The Mexicans had gathered several wild longhorns, and they slaughtered some of these and fed us. After we had eaten the meat, the soldiers then prepared us for another march by binding our wrists and ankles with strips of damp hide cut from the same cattle.

The intestines of the slaughtered animals were turned inside out and given to us to use for water vessels. We filled them and hung them around our necks, and as we resumed our marching, southward again toward that coppery sun, the sloshing of the water in those intestines made the same sound it must have made in the cattle, back when they had still been living.

And still our numbers kept diminishing. Two of our men, Priest Gibbons and Crandall Nash, crawled out from beneath the corral one night, sneaked into the water reserves, and drank all they could hold, and then died in agony a few hours later, their systems shocked into exploding.

The soldiers marched us toward the nearest jail, which was at Saltillo; we could not have made it all the way to the fort, the prison, at Hacienda del Salado. And even at that, it was a difficult march. Our captors were alternatively frustrated or made compassionate by our slow progress. One day a soldier might offer any of us a hand up, assisting us from a sitting position, when it was time to march again, and the next day the same soldier might give the same prisoner but a jaunty sneer, signifying the smug knowledge that no good end lay ahead for the captive. One day the soldiers would knock us sprawling to the ground with the butts of their muskets, and the next day they would be inquiring about our health, soliciting water and extra rations of food for us from the caravan's new leader, General Francisco Mejia. (In time-honored military tradition, Colonel Barragan had been busted down in rank for allowing us to escape.)

Some of the soldiers even got off their horses and walked so that the more emaciated of us could ride.

Our physician, Dr. Sinnickson, expired, falling off his horse as he did so, and it was a lonely feeling indeed, gathering around him and not knowing how to help him who had been helping us.

The pairings of history, the inescapable relationship between predator and prey; the way two oxen pull a plow so much more powerfully than one. I came slowly to understand that two of anything are required for the movement of history, and — no matter whether allies or combatants, friends or foes — there must be pairings. Otherwise, all is stillness, and latent powers lie unsummoned, like a planted field that receives no water.

After his defeat at San Jacinto, the Mexican president, Santa Anna, had been living in semiretirement at his Vera Cruz estate. Weary of battle, he was spending the bulk of his time raising enormous preening peafowl. He raised fighting gamecocks as well, which he would pit against one another in battles to the death.

Santa Anna had kept up a regular and, at times, warm correspondence with the general who had defeated him at San Jacinto, the Texas president, Sam Houston. It was Houston who had given Santa Anna back his freedom following his humiliating loss. (Shackled and hectored by the Texans after that battle, Santa Anna had tried to commit suicide with an overdose of laudanum. A Texas physician, James Phelps — whose son, Orlando, ironically, was still with us on this expedition — had pumped the poison from his stomach and cared for him afterward, until he could be released.)

Santa Anna would have been unlikely to order our execution without first consulting with Sam Houston, but Santa Anna was no longer always sentient, or available, disappearing for days at a time; in his absence he left the country to a fierce and impulsive associate, General Nicolás Bravo.

Bravo had been incensed to hear of our escape from Salado; when he heard that we had been recaptured, he had ordered us executed immediately.

General Mejia, who had been marching us down to Saltillo, detouring once again through all the little villages to show us off, refused to follow Bravo's orders. The word had not come directly from Santa Anna himself, and we were too pathetic: it would have been like crushing insects. It would have been murder, not war. His pride as a soldier would not allow him to do it. Mejia was transferred, and his subordinates — kinder than ever to us now, as if we were not hardened criminals but tottering old people — escorted us the rest of the way to the Saltillo jail.

Would we Texans have been as kind, as noble, were our positions to be reversed? It shamed me to consider that some of us might not.

In Saltillo we were shoved into little cells, stacked and jammed into dank cubicles like stock, officers and irregulars alike. We were fed once a day and not allowed to cleanse ourselves.

Charles Reese was in my cell, as well as other men I did not know. Each morning, for four days in a row, we awoke — if our fitful rest, amid so much tubercular hacking and groaning, could be called sleep — to find that a man had died in the night, though, alas, our cell never became more spacious, for no sooner was the deceased carried out than another (almost as sickly) was shoved in to replace him, taken from a cell that was evidently even more crowded, incredibly, than our own.

As men came to and went from our cell, and through a clandestine system of wall-tapping, we heard rumors. Whitfield Chalk and Caleb St. Clair had made it home and were agitating for our release. The situation was delicate, for the United States wished to annex Texas, even as Mexico still desired to reconquer Texas. Further complicating things, Great Britain — Mexico's friend — wished to remain friendly with the United States but did not want to see the United States become even more powerful by the annexation of so much territory.

The U.S. ambassador to Mexico, Waddy Thompson, had met with Santa Anna, arguing for our release, even as Santa Anna (whose hold on power in his own country was slipping fast) explained that he had to execute at least some, and perhaps all, of us. We had killed Mexican soldiers in our escape from Salado; retribution was demanded.

Sam Houston — cunning politician — had also been working for our release, but in a different way: not just for our own sake, but as leverage against both the United States and Mexico. While Waddy Thompson and the United States tried to intervene on our behalf, Sam Houston was appealing to Great Britain for help, so the British minister, Richard Pakenham, joined the discussion. Three countries were competing for our release. We were valuable as symbols even as we were all but worthless as men.

Thomas Jefferson Green — in the cell next to us — rapped out the message that if these things were true, then he hated our commander in chief, Sam Houston, and believed he was too little a soldier and too much a politician.

While negotiations for our freedom were taking place, one of our men, Billy Reese (brother of the reluctant-to-escape Charles Reese), was allowed to go down to Mexico City, because of his general intelligence and eloquence, to meet with Waddy Thompson and Pakenham.

Reese — who had heard Fisher read aloud to us countless times Sam Houston's tattered secret letter exhorting rebellion — found out from Thompson that in his letter to the British minister asking for our release, Houston had stated that we had marched into Mexico without orders.

Our little pissant expedition, begun with such high hopes for glory — indeed, sustained by the near-religious fervor that what we were doing mattered more than anything in the world — had crumbled. For a while we had felt powerful, significant, filled with life and meaning. Now we lay moaning with illness, wracked by pneumonia, on cold stone floors in a foreign country, while the world, we were to find out later, continued to argue over us as if we were stray poker chips.

Still, we fought, if only for our own lives. Still, some of us held on to hope.

We were not recovering. We were languishing. Occasionally another one or two men would be strained from out of the mountains and thrown back into the mix, gaunt and fevered. We were still receiving only one meal per day, though when we pointed out we were dying we were given an extra piece of bread and a ration of coffee to improve our spirits.

I held on to my beans more as talismans now than nutrition. For some illogical reason, I had it in my mind that when they were all gone I would be free, that however many beans I had left, that was how many days I had: but that I was allowed, by some unknown law of the world, to eat only one per day.

We had no blankets. The sound of coughing kept us awake all night. Sometimes we dozed in the daytime, when it was slightly warmer. One boy became deathly ill with pneumonia. When visited by a local padre who wished to administer last rites, he refused. He died three days later. This made some among us believe that if they accepted the Catholic faith, they might be rewarded with better treatment. They converted, but, alas, no special dispensation was forthcoming, save for the loathing and censure cast their way now by the rest of us.

In Mexico City, Santa Anna made his decision, though we were not to learn of it immediately. Certain of us would live, and certain of us would die.

After three weeks, Mejia's replacement, Colonel Ortiz, told us that we would be leaving the prison at Saltillo and would be marched south toward Mexico City, where we would be freed. We had heard by now of General Mejia's defiance of the initial order to execute us weeks earlier, and so we believed this wonderful news and were swayed by Colonel Ortiz's cheerful manner as he told us to walk fast, for we would soon be free men. Among us all, he said, only Fisher and Green would be punished — they were to be banished to the horrible Castle of Perve in the faraway town of Perote. Hearing this, we were sorry for the fate of our captains, though there were some among us also who, after our long months of captivity, during which time the captains had occasionally been squired and wined and dined, felt that things were evening out some, now. Still, we vowed to ourselves to lobby for their release upon our return to Texas.

On the first day of the march, when Ortiz saw that we were bothered by the dust kicked in our faces by the cavalrymen who rode alongside us, he ordered the riders to fall to the rear, leaving us out in front and alone, and for a short, glorious while, it felt as if we were free already.

It was but two long days' march to Hacienda del Salado, the site of our initial escape, and later on that second day, as we drew nearer to it, Ortiz's co-commander, Colonel Huerta, ordered us to stop, and placed our manacles back upon us.

The day was warm and sunny, but as we paused on the hill to look down at the old prison, a dark swirling cloud blew across the sun, a sudden sandstorm that completely obscured our view. We could not see our hands in front of our faces, and we cowered, then fell to the ground, seeking cover wherever we could: behind a log, in the scalloped lee of a dune, or even against one another.

Cursing, Ortiz and Huerta and the rest of their cavalry dismounted and hid behind their horses, trying to block the stinging sand. Jerking the manacled pack-train of us to our feet, they pushed us on.

We reached the walls of the prison, feeling them with our hands more than seeing them, and moved laterally in the blinding storm until we reached the gate and then entered, where the one hundred seventy-six of us encountered thirty well-armed infantrymen. As soon as we had entered the fort and were unmanacled, the storm stopped. And as we took our coats off, emptying the sand from our sleeves and shaking it from our bodies as if we had been deeply buried and had just emerged, we all noticed the terrible stillness and silence within the fort.

Through an interpreter, we were told only now of Santa Anna's decision to implement the *diezmo* to determine our fates. The terrible Colonel Huerta took pleasure in explaining that one out of every ten of us was going to be killed. "You came seeking glory but sacrificed your own freedom," the interpreter told us.

In a daze, I heard the words. *Libertad. Muerto.* The interpreter said something about blood and soil, but I was too weak to hear it all clearly.

"You will draw from a jar of black beans and white beans," the interpreter told us. "Some of you will draw the black bean of death," he said. "Others of you will draw a white bean and will be spared, if but a little longer." The interpreter — a young man not much older than myself, and seeming nervous in his uniform — related all of this in a calm voice, as if he were giving us directions to some long-sought destination only a short distance farther down the road. Colonel Huerta, however, was smiling wickedly.

We were all silent for a minute, stuporous. Then Cameron went berserk, charging the guards, followed by a small group around him, and the guards had to beat them back with the butts of their muskets.

Almost immediately, altar boys brought out an earthen crock and a bench. The crock was placed on the bench.

Colonel Huerta brought out a sack of white beans and counted out one hundred fifty-nine of them, one by one, speaking quietly in Spanish, dropping them into the clay pot as we watched. Then a smaller sack was brought to him — black beans — and from this sack he counted out seventeen and poured them in on top of the white beans, then shook the pot weakly in a thinly veiled attempt to keep the black beans of death near the top, as our officers and captains would be drawing first.

We were further surprised to see Shepherd again, standing among the fort's cavalrymen, though he no longer appeared to be in their ranks. He was bruised, beaten, and cowed, and the guards shoved him roughly toward us, making it clear that he, too, was expected to draw a bean.

All my life up to that point, I had been a conscious creature of restraint, more comfortable standing back and waiting and watching, observing things to the fullest extent possible before making a decision. I felt that this course was prudent, and it had usually served me well.

But there in the stone fort, when I saw Huerta counting, with pleasure, the white and black beans into the pot, I was lifted suddenly by a tremendous wave. All of my life's inaction had been but a quiet gathering for the action that was demanded now. I had been seized as if by a great storm, and I had no choice.

As the Mexican officers were posting sentries on the walls all around us, I sorted surreptitiously through my small handful of beans for the cleanest white ones I could find.

I could see no way, in the chaos of the moment, to gather and explain to all those for whom I cared deepest the nature of my surprising and secret bounty. In my first surge of panic, I had the thought that survival would be as easy as merely passing out white beans, and I started to do this, making a mental list, an awful prioritization of those whom I wanted to survive.

On the far side of our throng, I saw Charles McLaughlin, who even at this dire time was seated on an overturned saddle, sketching. I was alarmed to see that Cameron and Wallace were also over on the far side of the courtyard; I did not think there would be time to reach them.

Clearly the protection of Fisher and Green was my duty, one of my loyal obligations, and yet something in me counseled hesitation as I made my way toward them, and then I realized what it was. If any of the other men to whom I gave a white bean was to draw a black bean, and then discarded it, revealing the white bean I'd given him, the Mexicans' quota would be off. Whoever I handed a white bean would have also to somehow secretly drop two beans into the pot, even while they were reaching in to select another. Because there would be no chance to put one's hand into the pot a second time — to add another white or black bean to replace whatever color each prisoner had drawn honestly — we could only guess what those colors would be. Somehow, they had to add up to seventeen black beans. It was possible that by dropping another black bean in and revealing in the palm of one's hand the substitute white, there might end up being eighteen black beans in the pot. Perhaps General Huerta would think it possible that they had somehow miscounted, despite their painstaking care, but what would he make of nineteen or even twenty black beans drawn?

And if an eighteenth black bean did appear, from my sleight of hand — my assurance — that would mean my survival had come at the expense of not just one but two of my comrades.

The switchings required were too complex to explain to more than one person in the time remaining, and only I and possibly one other could get through the gate of life, even if only for a little while longer. I made my choice.

James Shepherd was standing off from the rest of us, shoulders hunched up in the big officer's coat he still wore, head tipped down, as if he were studying the soil in which he might soon be buried. He looked young again, younger even than he had been when he'd started out, and though he was diminished by the loss of his arm, he still possessed the handsomeness and elegance that had first caused the officers of both nations to take him in under their wing.

I hesitated, then hurried over and reached for his hand, took it, and pressed a white bean into his palm.

He looked down at it with no emotion that I could discern, and then looked back at me, and I saw with a shock that he was angry — and my breath caught, and I stared back at him, uncomprehending. Looking away from me then, he clenched the bean in his fist, then cast it to the ground fiercely.

I bent down quickly, picked it back up before anyone could see it, and pressed the bean upon him again, more urgently, saying, "You don't understand, this can get you home."

He looked at me again, more fiercely than before, and threw the bean down again.

Two guards came running up, thinking that we were about to fight, and separated us with the bayonets attached to their muskets, moving us back from each other and urging us into the line.

Colonel Huerta was moving among others of us, jabbing us with his bayonet. Huerta insisted that Cameron draw first. Cameron nodded, stepped out from the crowd, looked at us and smiled, then approached the clay pot.

His big crooked mason's hand was nearly too large to fit in the jar's mouth. He squeezed it through, stuck it all the way to the bottom, pulled it back out, examined his bean, and then grinned again. "Dig deep, boys," he called out.

Our officers drew next, one at a time: Fisher likewise drawing a white bean, as did Green. One of the men who had been an officer, a legitimate soldier in previous campaigns, a Captain Eastland, drew a black bean, and, stoically, he allowed himself to be separated from the rest of us. He sat on a bench, surrounded by soldiers, and watched the rest of us with clearly mixed emotions, wondering who his companions were to be.

After the last officer had drawn — all the others drew white — the rest of us were called forward to stand in line for life or death.

One of the sentries guarding the wall of the fort fainted and fell, like some plummeting angel, the gold tassels on his uniform fluttering as he flew to earth. His musket clattered to the ground, breaking when it landed, and there was a brief pause as the other soldiers revived him.

Colonel Huerta placed each white bean that was drawn in a little pile on a bench, in a patch of spring sunlight, and placed Captain Eastland's black bean and subsequent others in a vest pocket, as if they were some vital part of his essence that he had only loaned to the occasion, but from which he could not be long separated.

Henry Whaling's turn came. Even with the salvation of

my white bean held tight in my sweating hand, my own heart was pounding, and I could not imagine what it must be like for those who did not have a white bean already in their hand. What if I dropped mine, or lost it in the pot when I plunged my hand in? What if I was unsuccessful in the sleight-of-hand transfer and was caught?

Up ahead of me — his back turned to me — Henry Whaling was just standing there, staring down at his bean. Stoic as ever — though surely wishing for a second chance — he was led away to the bench.

I walked up to the pot, trying to look properly terrified: and I was. Never had I had so many eyes upon me. Hundreds of eyes, from all directions.

I stood at the pot for the longest time, and in the depth of that fear, I was tempted to not even try the trick: to play it straight, foolishly and recklessly, and to take my chances as had everyone else. As had Henry Whaling.

The odds were still good — not quite nine in ten — seventy men remained behind me, and eight black beans. It could even be argued that it would be safer to play it straight, for if I was discovered I would surely be executed with the rest.

One of the guards barked an order to draw, and I shook my head as if to clear it from a deep sleep and made the choice to choose life. With a black bean still in my right hand and my white bean in my left, I lowered my right hand into the pot, released my bean, rummaged blindly, selected two beans, and withdrew them, and then clasped both hands before my face with eyes shut, as if in prayer, in a manner I hoped would seem natural to the Catholic superstitions of the guards, and pretended to transfer the bean to my left hand. I lowered my right hand inconspicuously to my side, with its two unknown, just-drawn beans, and opened my left hand to show the guards — all eyes upon it — to reveal the old white bean I had been carrying for a month.

Tears sprang to my eyes, partly from the joy of being allowed to keep living, but partly at the cost — someone else, some seventeenth, and perhaps even an eighteenth among the seventy still behind me, would pay for my duplicity — and it was not until I was back among the crowd of the saved, over on the other side of the courtyard, that I even thought to examine the two beans I had drawn, the true beans: and when I did, I was astounded to see that, indeed, one was as black as coal.

Who would take my place? I could barely watch, and yet I could not turn my eyes away.

When it was Bigfoot Wallace's turn to pick, he walked up to the pot and pushed his big hand in and rummaged around for a maddeningly long time — examining each bean, it seemed.

He had been studying the proceedings as intently as any hunter, and he told us later that it seemed to him that the black beans were larger than the white. He rolled each bean in his fingers, determined to find the smallest one. When he finally found the tiniest one left and withdrew it, it was neither black nor white, but an indeterminate grayish swirl, and we all held our breath, awaiting the decision.

Huerta took the bean from him and examined it for a long time in that spring sunlight. He finally judged the bean to be white.

There was only one prisoner who seemed overcome by the

horror. This man, Patrick Altmus, was wringing his hands and moaning audibly, continually telling those near him that he would draw a black bean.

Altmus could not be summoned to his feet, and so the guards had to drag him over to the jar and force his hand into it. They told him to pick one and only one bean, and that if he drew more than one bean he would be shot with the others, regardless of the color of the beans.

He kept his hand in there a long time, before finally drawing a bean. His presentiment proved too true, for in it he held a fatal black bean. He turned deadly pale as his eyes rested upon it, and he turned and looked toward me, bewildered and terrified.

He uttered not another word and appeared resigned to his fate — as if the anticipation and dread had been the hard part, but now the dying would come easy.

When it was James Shepherd's turn to draw, he approached the urn with a swaggering indifference.

Although there were but five beans left and two of them had to be black, he barely bothered to look at his bean after he had drawn it — it was black, yet he seemed to give it no more mind than if it were a tick he had plucked from his pants cuff.

The four remaining irregulars approached the urn one by one. The first two selected white beans, as did the third, so that finally, it was George Washington Trahern who had to go through the motions of drawing with the foreknowledge that the bean within the pot was black. When he pulled it out, it was indeed black. He stared at it a long time, and then he was escorted over to join the other sixteen.

*   *   *

There was barely time for the condemned to pen last messages to their beloveds. On a scrap of parchment, and in shaking hand, Robert Dunham composed these final words:

> Dear Mother,
>
>   I write to you under the most awful feelings that a son ever addressed a mother, for in half an hour my life will be finished on earth, as I am doomed to die by the hands of the Mexicans for our latest attempts to escape. It was ordered by Santa Anna that every tenth man should be shot. We drew lots. I was one of the unfortunate. I cannot say anything more. I will die I hope with firmness. May God bless you, bless you, and may He in this last hour forgive and pardon all my sins . . . farewell.
>
>   Your affectionate son,
>   R. H. Dunham.

Henry Whaling insisted on a last meal, and the cooks prepared mutton and beans. Few of the other doomed men had any appetite, but Whaling gorged himself — had several bowls of the very type of beans that had determined the end of his life — then called for a cigar, which he smoked slowly, with apparent satisfaction.

The doomed were marched to a courtyard on the opposite side of the wall. A priest who had been marching with us since Saltillo sprinkled holy water on the ground where they were about to die and offered to administer last rites. Only two of the seventeen accepted.

It was dusk: poor shooting light. A log had been placed along the wall of the corral and nine men seated on it to be executed; the other eight would wait their turn.

The rest of us were kept under heavy guard on the other side of the courtyard's wall. We could see nothing but heard everything.

It took a lot of shooting — volley after volley, amid much shouting. One of our surviving white bean Texans, William Preston Stapp, wrote later:

> The wall against which the condemned were placed was so near us we could hear every order given in arranging the work of death.
>
> The murmured prayers of the kneeling men stole faintly over to us — then came the silence that succeeded, more eloquent than sound —
>
> — Then the signal taps of the drum — the rattle of muskets, as they were brought to aim — the sharp burst of the discharge, mingled with the shrill cries of anguish and heavy groans of the dying, as soul and body took their sudden and bloody leave.

Soldiers standing guard atop the fort's ramparts had turned to watch the executions, and again, some of them began to swoon, falling to the ground.

We heard later that mutton-eating Henry Whaling died as well as any man or woman might ever hope. The Mexicans kept shooting but couldn't kill him. And while they were shooting at him, Henry Whaling sat and cursed them.

The remaining eight waited and listened to him, as did the rest of us: as did I, with his bean, the extra bean, sitting unused in my pocket.

Whaling absorbed more than a dozen shots, and still he kept hollering and cursing, and the Mexicans kept shooting — they ran out of bullets and had to stop and reload, listening all the while to his bellowings — and then began firing again.

His entrails were spilling from him. The black beans he had eaten were spilling back out onto the soil, undigested. He kept shouting.

Finally Huerta walked across the courtyard in that dim light, put his pistol to Whaling's temple, and fired.

The nine dead were then dragged away and stacked like cordwood in a corner of the corral, and the other eight were summoned — in the darkness, now — and the job was finished: again, crudely and inefficiently.

There was one among the seventeen who escaped. James Shepherd had somehow survived. One musket ball had blown through his cheek and another had fractured his arm, but he had never lost consciousness, and had lain there blood-covered in the stack of sixteen dead men, pretending to be dead himself while the village dogs chewed on the dead men's arms and feet and legs and licked the sticky blood from their bodies.

That night, after the sentries had fallen asleep, Shepherd crawled away. It was not until the next day during burial duty that the soldiers discovered seventeen had become sixteen and realized he was missing. When we survivors heard of it, we cheered, until Huerta informed us that if he was not found, one of us would take his place.

The soldiers followed his blood trail out of the fort, but they lost it when it disappeared into the mountains, taking the same grueling path Cameron and his followers had attempted in our first escape.

He wandered, we learned later, for four days, before someone recognized him and turned him in. He was taken to the outskirts of town and shot again, this time for good. By then we were already a hundred miles away, manacled and bound in chains, marching south once more.

5

THE TACUBAYA ROAD

WE AWAKENED AT dawn, haunted by the horrors of the day before.

Following breakfast, we were chained, and we filed past the outer wall of the courtyard where the victims still lay piled, as William Preston Stapp was to write later from his cell at Perve, with their "stiffened and unsepulchered bodies, weltering in blood . . . their rigid countenances, pallid and distorted with agony."

The weakest of us were allowed to ride in oxcarts, and though many of us were still at death's door, not fully recovered from our time in the mountains, the younger and stronger began to improve as we moved slowly across the central plateau and into the more fertile and heavily populated regions north of Mexico City. The villages were so frequent now that we almost always were able to spend the night under a roof, in an abandoned silo or barn, and now and again we were allowed a day of rest, as well as more frequent baths. When we reached the city of San Luis Potosí, nearly five hundred miles from the border now, we were allowed to take our chains off, nearly a month after we had departed Salado.

In San Luis Potosí, we left five of our number behind in a hospital — they all soon died — and three more died of pleurisy soon after we resumed the march toward Mexico City.

In the smaller towns, such as Queretaro and San Miguel, the townspeople, chagrined at our raggedness, would often take up small collections on our behalf — though horribly impoverished themselves — in order to allow each of us to buy an extra bowl of beans or extra cup of *pulque*, the latter which relaxed us considerably and made us feel, for a while, that we were not in such a bad place after all, and that where we were bound for might yet be better than where we had been.

We rested again in the village of Tula, where Colonel Ortiz was finally relieved of us and a new escort took over. Most of us were beginning, finally, to feel stronger, and were beginning, once more, to talk at night in low murmurs of trying to escape again.

The next day we reached the even tinier village of Huehuetoca, and upon our arrival another sandstorm came from out of nowhere, every bit as inexplicable and fierce as the one that had marked our entrance to the fort of Salado.

That night, a lone express rider arrived from the south, having ridden hard from Mexico City, with the news that Ewen Cameron was to be taken from us and shot the next morning. Alfred Thurmond, who had been serving as our translator when needed, was allowed to sit with Cameron in his stone cell the last few hours until daylight, at which time the rest of us were pushed southward. Thurmond rejoined us by noon of that same day.

We had not been gone ten minutes, Thurmond said, when Cameron was taken outside and ordered to stand against a stone wall. The cavalry surrounding him dismounted and took aim at extremely close range. The tips of their muskets were wavering, Thurmond said.

Cameron refused to accept the blindfold that was offered him and instead bared his chest, glaring at the executioners, and called on them to fire.

He died instantly, Thurmond said, shredded by musket fire, and Thurmond wept. Of the giants, only Bigfoot Wallace now remained among us.

Months later we were to learn that Cameron had been executed because — according to Mexico's minister of war, José Maria Tornel — he had been "one of the most active Partisans in the warfare going on between the two countries," and because, whenever imprisoned, he had ceaselessly encouraged fellow prisoners to escape. While they were at it, they had piled on a great list of other offenses — some purely fabricated, others, perhaps, closer to the truth.

We mourned him for days, on the trail to Mexico City — though he had never been an officer, he, more than anyone, had been our leader, particularly in times of deepest trouble. Now that he was gone, we were all diminished and weakened, and our spirit burned less brightly.

It felt to all of us, I think, as if the landscape were swallowing us now — as if we were descending, mile by mile, day by day, into a pit so vast and deep that we would never be able to get out again.

We came into the valley of Mexico City two days after Cameron's death and saw immense and shining lakes in all directions, the great bodies of water on which the Aztecs had once built floating gardens. We were humbled to be in the presence of so hallowed and powerful a civilization, and by the audacity of our own puny notions, eight hundred miles earlier, that our little band could mount a successful assault on such a glorious and ancient nation.

The volcanoes Popocatépetl and Ixtaccíhuatl ringed the valley, and many of us saw snow for the first time, in the glaciers that capped their peaks. Our ultimate destination, the Castle of Perve, was in the southernmost tip of the country. We still had hundreds of miles to go to reach it, but because we were so threadbare (Bigfoot Wallace, in particular, was indecent to the point that he had to wear his broad floppy hat like a loincloth, and to protect his head from the sun he used a single red bandanna, wrapped like a turban), and because there was a road that needed rebuilding, and because our new escorts still desired, like all the others, to try to bask a bit in the glory of having captured us, we remained in Mexico City, at the prison of Molino del Rey, working in a quarry and rebuilding the ancient road to Tacubaya. In exchange for our labor, we would be given one new set of clothes each.

From the quarry each day, we cut and hauled slabs of white stone, square-cut rectangles of pleasing shape and density and texture. As we sledged them free with hammer and pry bar, the acid odor of rock dust that attended each stone's separation from the main body of the quarry was like the burned odor of a musket just fired; and, occasionally, after some certain slab's successful cleaving, I would be reminded of Shepherd and his lost arm.

The work was little different from the backbreaking labor we would have been doing at home — wielding shovels and swinging sledgehammers and grubbing hoes, hauling water and stone — but soon the men turned into the most awful laggards I have ever witnessed. Having been given our one new set of clothes — flannel one-piece prison uniforms striped red and white and green, and sandals (Bigfoot Wallace's had to be custom-made), most of the men began almost immediately to stall the project's progress in whatever way they could.

There was a major regret from that time, beyond the regret of having gone to war in the first place. I met a girl my own age, and think that I fell in love with her. I believe I would have traded my life for hers — would have traded this long life even, for more time with her — and I believed, and still believe, that she would have done the same.

She was the daughter of the architect who had been commissioned to design and rebuild the road, Colonel Raul Bustamente. He awakened us each morning at dawn, treated us with dignity and respect, and trusted us to work as perhaps he himself would have worked had he been in our position. We were paired in chains with ten feet separating us — I found myself partnered with Charles McLaughlin — and we walked each morning from the stone prison at Molino del Rey to the new road on the outskirts of the city.

It was a pleasant walk in the cool of the morning. It was early spring, and the countryside all around us was leaping into green, the birds singing. We walked with the excess footage of our ankle chains hooked to our belts and wrapped around our waists to keep them from dragging. And compared to the previous days of our captivity, and all the ones that were to follow, I have to say that I remember those days as being the most pleasant.

It was on this path that I first saw Clara, Bustamente's daughter, crossing the road — or what passed for a road — with her friends on their way to school, though I wasn't to learn she was his daughter for quite some time. The girls were dressed in bone white uniforms, and as we stopped to let them pass — half a dozen of them — the dust we had been raising with our trudging rose higher and caught up with us, surrounding us as we stood there. The dust was the same color as their dresses, and as it rose around us I could taste it.

We stood there like cattle, or a herd of horses, with Bustamente at the front, his hand held up in a signal for us to halt. The girls were a good distance in front of us — thirty or forty yards — and he intended to keep it that way.

As they crossed, they glanced our way and waved to him, and Bustamente nodded back, but the girl kept looking at us, peering at our faces as if searching for someone she knew. She watched me for a moment — never had I felt so *found* — and then she was gone.

The chalk dust from the road was still settling around us. It landed, fine as fog or mist, on the hair on our arms, our faces, our eyebrows: the finest powder imaginable, stone crushed to a substance one step away from invisible, by nothing more than the simple footsteps of tens or even hundreds of thousands of others just like us, marching back and forth through the centuries — to market, to school, to church, to death — and by the iron and hide and wooden wheels of *carettas*, from countless other such passages, and by the hooves of the beasts that had pulled them: donkey, ox, and horse.

The girls, the young women, were long gone. Colonel Bustamente's arm was still raised in the halt position, as if to counsel us not to even speak of what we had seen. Finally he lowered his hand slowly, took a newly starched linen handkerchief from his pocket, and wiped the street dust from his face, and then we proceeded on, north. As we passed the place where the young women had crossed in front of us, I looked in the direction they had gone, seeking to memorize the buildings and alleys, the landscape and terrain.

I scanned the dust to the side of our passage, searching for their tracks, and did not realize I was lingering until I felt the tug of the chains lurching me back into the procession, and was nudged simultaneously by Charles McLaughlin.

I stumbled, was pulled along. The men in front of me glanced back in confusion and some irritation, and I stepped back into their haunted flow — *glory*, they had said they wanted, each of them — with a secret burning in my heart. I carried it with me all the rest of the day.

Charles McLaughlin laughed, watching my initial stumbling. "You would not like it if I were to draw a portrait of the young man in love," he said. "You would be horrified by your appearance," he said.

We walked in silence a while, with me feeling both mortified and exhilarated, and a little farther down the road, McLaughlin spoke again: "Better by a hundred your chances of slipping free of these chains, being given an officer's horse, and riding uncontested all the way back to Texas, than ever seeing that girl again, much less ever speaking to her, much less ever holding her in your arms, much less . . ."

His voice trailed off into a laugh of utter delight, and I blushed and said nothing, but after we had walked quite a bit farther I said, "You're wrong," and he smiled after that, and did not argue.

Each day, Bustamente directed us to a wide and shallow stream far outside of town, from which we were to gather decorative rocks for the road. The chalky square-cut quarry was the source for our paving stones, but it was this stream that yielded the finer, prettier rocks for the project. He called it Rio Seco, the dry river, though it was not dry that spring. Judging by the boulders it had moved, sun-bleached and round, and by the scatter of driftwood, the water-polished assemblage of giant cottonwoods piled into fantastic clumps of debris, it was evident that huge torrents of water had cascaded down the floodplain not long ago, transporting the rattling, clattering boulders and great hollowed-out cottonwood spars. Scatters of giant stone, boulders as big as houses, were nestled in amid cobbles the size of a man's fist. Our task was to select the most attractive, ornamental river stones and carry them, along with the bags of the valuable white river sand, all the way back to the road.

Working at the river, we had slightly more freedom. It was nearly an hour's walk down a steep trail to the river bottom, and our small gang — McLaughlin, myself, and a dozen other recruits, all young men, stronger and healthier than the rest — soon reached a tacit understanding with the guards that we would not run away and they would not have to descend and then ascend with us each time we went down the steep path to the river. I poured my energies into the hauling, so I often did the work of three or four men — accumulating a greater stack of boulders on the days when we went down to the Rio Seco, or cutting and laying more stone on quarry days. The guards and Bustamente noticed my work, although Bustamente almost always stayed up on the road, two miles distant, after having taken us down to the river only that first day, wandering out among the tangled cataclysm of stone to show us what kinds of rocks he preferred.

The river was brilliant and heated, dazzling. But on the riverbanks beneath the ash, cottonwood, and sycamore trees, it was green and cool and shady, with the leaves fluttering in the spring wind, and it was easy to lie in the white sand and listen to the wind in the tops of the trees and to imagine that in another life the stonemason Ewen Cameron might have enjoyed working with the Rio Seco's stones, even as another part of me knew there was at least as much chance that had he remained living, he would be using these very stones to try to bash in the heads of our captors.

Not all of the boneyard of the river was parched. In some places a ribbon of water still trickled through the riverbed's center, running and then pooling before disappearing for a while, only to reemerge elsewhere. Cool breezes bathed these wetted portions of the canyon and rose from the sparkling, riffling water scented with the growth of new life. Tiger-striped butterflies and those the colors of emeralds and amethysts gathered in great numbers by the salty riverside puddles to sip before rising into a flashing kaleidoscope of escape, each one a tornado of broken church glass, frightened by our own sweating, salty, labored approach.

Out among the boulders, our footing was uncertain and we slipped often. We jettisoned the boulders when we could — sometimes they cracked in half when they landed — though other times we could not turn loose of them quickly enough and smashed our arms and thumbs and fingers, so that the river canyon echoed with the sound of curses, and the stones and boulders were smeared and painted with the bright red palm prints of such mishaps, as were some of the stones that would ultimately go into the road above.

Still, all in all it was a place of peace, not just for me but for each of us. Bright songbirds of every color were drawn to the water and the leafy foliage that grew alongside the river. Wild roses bloomed on gravel-bar islands and between the boulders, existing seemingly on nothing more than the rocks themselves, and air. Hummingbirds whirred about the blossoms, probing.

The cottonwood spars lined both banks, marking where the river had been, and served as impromptu benches for whenever we took a break, which, for the other workers, was increasingly often. I noticed that each of them was lulled into a state of great sleepiness and contentment by the sound of the river. The morning and afternoon light that passed through the riverside foliage cast a shimmering green on their faces, and sometimes they would lie down on various of the cottonwood spars, after searching for and finding the one polished spar that most perfectly fit the length and shape of their bodies: the curves and hollows and tapers of each spar determining to some extent the position of repose into which the prisoners settled.

The soldiers lay as if stupefied, nestled into the slick fit of their various logs, the men and logs both looking like the carcasses of giant fish that had washed ashore. They smoked precious cigarettes they had been able to purchase or to re-assemble from the scraps of butts gathered roadside, and when those were gone they cut crooked lengths of grapevine and smoked those, inhaling the thick sour smoke until they were nearly intoxicated and the riverside was filled with the blue haze of their exhalations. It was not unlike the scene of a battlefield, with the fallen soldiers, arms outflung and faces vacant to the sun, and the earth beneath them torched, and the smoke of cannonade still lingering; and if they did not know bliss, in those moments, they seemed at least to know peace.

The laggards napped briefly, or stared unblinking at the sky, while I continued to work and while Charles McLaughlin sketched. (Afterward, he kept his drawings, the evidence of our turpitude, rolled up inside his shirt; and even back at the garrison, where we were being housed, he did not display them, to keep from informing the other prisoners of the sweet details that attended our assignment.)

My coworkers would lounge there as long as they dared — an hour or sometimes even two — just long enough to make the guards watching the main crew back at the road become exasperated and consider sending someone after us, but not quite so long that they'd actually do it. We kept a lookout posted in the trees, watching the path down to the river, so that he could run and alert us to resume working if he saw anyone approaching.

One day, unknown to us, Charles McLaughlin's hidden charcoal sketches were discovered, with their damning portrayals of our indolence: the glee of the truants sharing stalks of grapevine, the contented smiles of the slumberers. The evidence, too, of my own ambitious labors, making my way through the boneyard of a river with both arms wrapped around a boulder as large as my chest, with the veins in my arms, neck, and forehead leaping out like deltas and rivers themselves.

The next day, after allowing us an hour's head start, Colonel Bustamente sent a pair of guards down the trail to check on us.

Our sentry that day was Daniel Drake Henrie, who had already fallen asleep at his post, and, having been somewhat an acolyte of Ewen Cameron, upon being discovered — upon being interrupted from a most pleasant dream, he was to tell us later — he responded not with shame and guilt but insolence, hurling insults at the two guards.

Down on the river, the sleeping men awoke from their naps and looked up to see the guards beating Daniel Henrie with their musket butts, clubbing him to the ground and then continuing to strike at him — no dream this, now. As it appeared they were likely to kill him, we charged up the trail with our shovels and pickaxes, twenty of us in chains versus two of them with but single-shot muskets and small derringers suited for little more than killing squirrels or rats. The guards backed away from the bruised and bleeding Henrie and hurried off for reinforcements.

Some of the men were all for breaking our chains and trying another escape, fearing we would be executed, while others of us thought we would merely be punished, and argued moderation, counseling that we would not be executed yet, for Bustamente still needed us to complete the road.

"If they try to whip me, I will kill them," Henrie said. "I will not let a Mexican whip me."

In the end we remained where we were — we did not go back down to the river to work, but waited at the top of the trail for the new muster of guards to come hurrying back — and when they arrived, twenty strong, shouting and firing their muskets, we stood our ground, fearing the worst.

They surrounded us, jabbing at Henrie with their bayonets, but did not strike him again, and instead escorted us roughly up the trail, back to Bustamente's road.

The work groups were changed after that — only Charles McLaughlin and I were allowed to remain on river duty — and not only were we allowed to keep traveling to the river with the new workers, but we had our chains removed as well, so that I was free to range as far as I wished in search of the most beautiful stones and boulders, while Charles McLaughlin was free to continue his sketches and document the various stages in the fruition of Bustamente's grand dream. Bustamente alternated McLaughlin between the river and the road, and the canyon and the quarry.

Just as McLaughlin had a haunting eye for detail in his illustrations, I was developing an eye for stone, not merely seeking the most interesting individual boulders — a stone the precise size and shape of a skull, complete with two water-worn sockets where the eyes would have been, only slightly off-kilter; a long slab shaped like a park bench, requiring the heft of four men; a boulder curiously shaped like the nation of Mexico, and another, lying not all that far away, even more curiously shaped like Texas — but also developing an aptitude for the placement of one rock against another. I traveled farther and farther upstream, searching for finer and more curious rocks, ranging for hours at a time — spending half a day sometimes, to return with only one good stone, and downstream, too, passing beneath the leafy green canopy of sunlit bower and birdsong.

The road was beginning to achieve a brilliance that not even Bustamente had imagined, with the thread of fantastic stones running like a seam through the predetermined elegance and simplicity of his design, and Bustamente — a man of integrity and generosity — gave me credit for my small share of the work. He saw me as the kind of man he wanted to believe we were all capable of becoming — transformed, under the benevolent shaping hands of the superior landscape and culture of Mexico, into men more civil, dignified, genteel. For a while, I even believed it myself.

She found me on the river two weeks later. She and her friends came to the river to wash their laundry. I had been working in a downstream stretch of the river that week — had discovered a seam of red boulders that crossed the river like the transverse slice of a knife across a piece of fruit — and I had petitioned Colonel Bustamente for the use of, and had received, a heavy iron pike with which to extricate some of the fractured stones from within this band. I was stacking and sorting them on the bank to dry in the sun.

I had followed the seam of red rock out into the sun-warmed boulder field where the river had once been, and was striking at a melon-shaped stone that seemed perfect for the fit I was envisioning. It was a lot of work for one rock, and the labor consisted mainly of pulverizing the surrounding jigsaw grip of the other rocks all around it. Each time I struck a rock with the heavy pike, the canyon echoed with the sound of the blow, cold iron against hot stone, and little sparks tumbled from the rock like flashing windblown blossoms. The scent and taste of burnt rock dust was dense around me. I liked the smell, and I liked working steadily, rhythmically, encouraging the earth to give up that one stone, though there were enough pauses in my work — stopping to take my damp shirt off to hang it over a creosote bush to dry, mopping the stinging sweat from my eyes with the crook of my arm, looking up at the dizzying distant sight of a caracara circling high above on a heated updraft from the same rocks in which I labored, as if in an oven — for anyone who heard my sledgings to know that it was a human who toiled and not a machine.

She and her friends had chosen a place farther downstream, but hearing the noise she walked upstream nearly a mile to find me. I saw her from a long way off. She had been advancing whenever I was occupied with the sledge, then pausing whenever I stopped — but even as I was working I noticed from the corner of my vision the uneven movement, the advancement, of her white dress against the riverside cottonwoods. Thinking at first that the white was the uniform of one of Bustamente's guards sent to spy on me, I kept working.

But I saw as she drew closer that she was a woman, then a young woman, and then I saw that it was her, and even though the rock was almost out — one or two more blows — I stopped, sweat-drenched and breathing hard, like a horse, and I leaned against the iron staff of the pry bar and waited for her to come that final distance.

"El constructor de caminos," she said, smiling. She looked around. *"Donde está tu camino?"*

We talked for an hour, mostly about the routine details of her life — her schooling, her family, her chores and tasks — but also about the larger abstractions, our loves and fears and beliefs.

She had learned nearly as much English from her father as I had Spanish from my captors, and she let me know quickly that she thought it was awful that we were having to work as slaves.

And yet, she said, for certain crimes and sins, there needed to be punishment.

"It's not the colonel's fault," I told her. "He's actually pretty good to us. He's treated us better than anyone else so far." I shrugged. "We chose to come into your country."

Her eyes sought mine. "Why?" she asked.

"I don't know," I said. I wanted to make a joke of it and say something like *To see you,* but I was seized with an over-whelming sadness.

"How many men have you killed?" she asked. Not *Have you killed any?* but *How many?*

I shook my head and looked away. "I can't remember who I was before I came across the river," I said.

She started to say something, but we heard voices, the sound of her friends coming to search for her, having be-come worried when they could no longer hear the sound of the iron bar against the stones. They paused by my cairn of red rocks some distance away from where Clara and I were sitting by the riverbed, and waited, and watched. She rose, dusted the grit from her dress, and asked if I would be here the next day.

"I can try," I said. "I will tell the colonel I need more red rocks." I looked around at the garden of stone, an eternity of stone.

She laughed — her teeth seemed large, framed by that smile — and holding her skirt above her ankles she walked carefully through the boulders, back to where her friends were waiting. When she reached them she smiled again and waved.

I watched them until they were gone, and only then did the sound of my sledging return to the canyon, as I still tried to pry free from the earth that one perfect stone, and then the next.

I worked until dusk, until the first fireflies began to appear and the tree frogs in the reeds and groves of cottonwoods began to trill, and the bullfrogs began their nighttime drumming. I was supposed to be back up on the road by that time and was still an hour's walk away, but it did not matter, this one evening: Colonel Bustamente trusted me.

Back at our garrison that first night, I told Charles McLaughlin what had happened. He said that all the other men, including Colonel Bustamente, believed that I had simply fallen asleep from having worked so hard; and it was not until I urged him to let the others continue to believe that story that he began to think I was telling the truth.

I visited with him about her for a long time — relayed not just the bits and pieces of our broken conversation — the general trading of news about siblings, friends and family, life histories, likes and dislikes. The words "truth" and "liberty" and "justice" were easily translatable across the two languages — *verdad, libertad, justicia* — but it had taken a bit more work to discuss our mutual admiration for other qualities such as courage, beauty, and the strength of one's heart. There were at least two kinds of strength, we had agreed, looking at the pile of red stones I had assembled; at least two.

"Do you love her?" Charles McLaughlin wanted to know. "Are you falling in love with her?"

"Yes," I said, answering the second question first, and then the first. "No. I don't know. It's that, but something more, something else. I don't know what," I said. "I don't know what it is."

"But it's everything, isn't it?" he asked. "It consumes you, like you're on fire, always burning?"

"Yes," I said, "that's what it's like. Have you known that feeling?"

He looked down at the sketch he was working on. "I have, and still do," he said. He brushed an eraser crumb from his sketch, then furrowed his brow, frowned, and touched his pencil to the page. It was a sketch of the fort, our jail. "That's not love," he said, still studying his sketch, so that at first he appeared to be speaking of his illustration. "That's obsession. Still, it'll certainly get you out of bed in the morning."

Though I hurled myself at the work, most of the men continued to resist. They cut slits into their bags so that as they ferried sand and gravel and cobble from the river to the road they left behind a sifting, wandering trickle, sometimes arriving at their destination with less than half a bag. Some of the men feigned injury or illness, though the Mexicans dealt with that by treating them universally with a diet of corn-meal gruel and castor oil, taking their clothes away, and confining them to a hospital bed, while outside the spring winds continued to rattle and the leaves shimmered in the sunlight.

Colonel Bustamente, exasperated, resisted the calls from his superiors to impose even harsher discipline, and instead tried to implement incentives to reward good workers, such as being fitted with lighter chains, or even having their chains removed completely. And it surprised me, if not him, that the men's work did improve, as did the quality of the road, which was drawing still more praise from Bustamente's superiors, all to his credit.

She did not show up the next day, or the next. Never had I felt so captive. A week passed like a century, and then another. I felt sure that she would find me again — would come walking back up the riverbank, picking her way through the bleached field of rocks and into the skein of red rocks.

And as I waited, I set about building her a gift of sorts: a little house, scarcely larger than a hut. I built it with the best stones I could find. There were various minerals in the riverbed — tiny flakes and nuggets of fool's gold, copper and silver, as well as reddish crystals that might have been rubies and garnets — and I made a rough mortar of clay and sand and inlaid the windows and doorjambs with these discoveries. The walls were dry stone. I fitted the stones together tightly, in a way that was pleasing and calming to the eye, and made a snugly latticed roof using the polished spars of driftwood. Numerous of the limbs and branches of the cottonwoods, in particular, seemed nearly indestructible, with green sprouts and buds and branches continuing to grow from the main corpse of the limb, even after so rough a downriver journey, and by watering the latticework of the roof I was able to encourage these sucker-sprouts to continue growing, so that they wrapped around one another like vines, binding the roof even more tightly. Soon the thatched covering was shaded with the newly emergent leaves of those horizontal cottonwood spars, as well as the dappled shadow-and-light cast from those trees still standing beside the small house.

I made a bed inside the hut, using driftwood slats cushioned with moss and leaves. My stonework blended so well with the natural, jumbled stone chaos of the floodplain, and the thatched roof merged so well with the riverside forest, that the tiny house was barely noticeable from a distance, even to my own eye. Sometimes I would find myself looking right at it without realizing I was seeing it. Small birds fluttered amid the leaves of the roof, flew out over the thin ribbon of the river's shallow center and hovered, angel-like, daring and snapping at rising hatches of aquatic insects.

I worked hard to finish up the tiny house, and harder still after I had it finished, never resting for more than a few minutes, so that she might know always where I was by the ringing-steel sound of my labor. I waited. All my life, I have waited.

Charles McLaughlin and I agreed how ironic it seemed that in having crossed the border "to stir up the whirlwind of war," we had ended up doing far more building up than tearing down; and of how, rather than leaving lamentations and ruin in our wake, we had a legacy of fine craftsmanship, such as the new thoroughfare we were working on, the rebuilt Ciudad Mier, and Charles McLaughlin's art.

In the evenings, McLaughlin sketched while I read, teaching myself Spanish in the process, asking our guards the names for certain words and phrases. *Forever. Desire. Meet me.* Little house, *casita.* Under the new system of rewards, nearly all of the Texans were allowed to travel into town in the evenings in small groups for dinner and entertainment, with only a single guard, but Charles McLaughlin and I usually stayed home, weary from our labors and content to sketch and read. While in town, one of our men, Matthew Pilkington, was caught in the embrace of an officer's wife, and was beaten severely; another was stabbed in the buttocks with an ice pick.

Many nights the guards had to carry drunk prisoners home on their shoulders, but Samuel Walker and a few of his more fiery compatriots, still intent on escape, always refrained from drinking. Walker inspired one prisoner, Willis Coplan, to simply walk away on the evening of July 30. The guards did not even notice he was missing — they called roll only once a day, in the evenings before the trips to town — and Samuel Walker now knew that he had less than twenty-four hours to attempt his own escape, knowing that once Coplan was discovered missing we would all be chained back together again and our privileges would be rescinded.

Walker resolved to leave the next evening, just before roll call, and spent the night tearing and knotting bed sheets with two of his best friends, James Wilson and D. H. Gattis.

Just before dusk, Walker and Wilson and Gattis walked past some Mexican soldiers, conversing earnestly, as if merely out for a stroll. They had hidden the knotted sheets by one of the fort's back walls in a tiny grove of shade trees, and as the summer dusk fell they scaled the walls with the bed sheets and let themselves over the other side.

They broke into a run, not even bothering to reel in their line of knotted sheets, and six other men, emboldened by the sight of their escape, climbed the wall and ran after them.

Willis Coplan, pursued almost incessantly by cavalry, traveled eight hundred miles, all the way back to the Rio Grande, only to be caught in that last hundred yards as he attempted to cross; he spent the next twenty years in captivity in Matamoros, within sight of the Texas border.

Samuel Walker, James Wilson, and D. H. Gattis also were captured, only a mile outside of Mexico City, but Walker paid their captors a dollar each and they were released. The next night they were captured again but were held in a one-room jail with a dirt floor. Using a wooden plank, they dug an opening beneath the door and slithered out.

Unlike Coplan, they headed for the coast, traveling alternately south and east, staying in the mountains, moving toward the scent of the ocean, where they hoped to be able to find an American vessel and sign on as deck hands.

Near a small mining village, they were apprehended again, but they pretended to be British mine workers. When asked for some sort of identification, James Wilson pulled out a wrinkled piece of paper on which a prisoner back at Molino del Rey had scribbled for him the words to an ancient ballad, "When Shall We Three Meet Again" — a song Wilson had been much taken by — and pretending to read from it, he cribbed a ludicrous declaration of passport that nonetheless convinced the cavalry, none of whom could read English.

Wilson fell ill after that and had to be left behind — no one ever saw him again — and Walker was recaptured yet again, but Gattis continued on, reaching Tampico a week later, where the United States consul was able to get him on a ship headed north.

Although there was a part of us that was happy for those who escaped, there was also a part of us resentful at the price we were made to pay for our compatriots' freedom. All of our privileges were revoked immediately, and we were put back in shackles and chains. Colonel Bustamente was nearly court-martialed over the incident, and he told us he had been given only one more chance by his superiors; that if another Texan escaped, Bustamente would be not only court-martialed, but also possibly executed. There were those in government, he said, who resented and disagreed completely with not only the tender treatment he had shown us but the fact that we were alive at all; that with the *diezmo*, nine in ten of us had evaded the call of justice.

"My life is in your hands," he said, speaking to us before dinner one evening. "I will be frank with you: Next to my family, this road is my life. Next to my family, this road is how I will be judged in the world, and is how I will judge myself. Another escape and I am gone, and the road will fall into lesser hands. I cannot afford that," he said, gesturing to our chains. "When the road is finished, on the other hand . . ." He made a gesture of both ambiguity and hope. "Perhaps then I will have more influence. Perhaps then I can be your patron and argue for your release."

What he said next caused some of us to wonder at first if he had been drinking; but I saw that he was cold sober.

"I will remain kind to you *soldados*," he said. "It is what is in my soul, this belief that all men should be equals — right up until the time you betray me, at which point I shall kill any of you without remorse.

"It is for my own safety that I imprison you all in the chains again," he said. "For that, I am sorry. But it is a small thing, for my own safety, and for what the road requires."

So once more Charles McLaughlin and I were chained together, which hampered his drawing, and my own reading; it made the road work more difficult, as well.

I was nearly frantic to return to the stretch of river where I had been quarrying the red stones and where I had built the *casita*. But after only a few days, during which we hauled out all the neatly stacked piles I'd gathered and laid the thin red ribbon of them in the road, in subtle patterns that were almost floral in nature, Bustamente suggested that he would like me to find another color of rock, and another style. *"Este verde,"* he said, holding up a fist-sized stone and pointing in the opposite direction from where I had been working. He said there was a seam of it that bisected the river upstream, just as the formation of red rock crossed downstream.

I told him I wanted to keep working the red rocks, and that I thought the road would be improved by having more of them, but he just laughed and said that no, that was the end of the red rocks.

Charles McLaughlin and I had only twenty feet of chain. He had to shield his face as I worked the sledge, to keep the rock chips from spraying him. There was not much to sketch. Often he would want to wander off into the shade to draw a certain tree, a certain scene, but I would want to remain out in the riverbed, pounding the green rocks, so that she might hear me working and might find me. My hands were calloused from gripping the sledge, and my shoulders bruised and swollen from the relentless jarring.

It had occurred to me that even if she did find me it might be awkward with Charles McLaughlin in attendance, and I had already resolved, should such a reunion occur, to break our chains, for that one day only, with the sledge bar, and then plead to Bustamente that it had been a mistake, that Charles McLaughlin had shifted just as I had been bringing the sledge down and that the chain had gotten in the way.

Bustamente liked me, Bustamente needed me. I felt certain I could get away with it once.

I did not like how the road looked now, with its abrupt transition from red to green, but Bustamente did. His guards were harsher to us and Bustamente was no longer friendly. His eyes glittered with what I presumed at the time was fear — the way we, the prisoners, ironically held sway over his own freedom, even his life — though I understand now it might have been more anger than fear.

In the early summer heat the manacles would grow unbearable, and we would plead with the guards to pour water over the iron, briefly cooling it. The shackles burned some men's legs like brands. Several men's wounds became infected, and a few men died and were buried in the little military cemetery by the shady grove within the fort's walls, near the spot where Samuel Walker and the others had climbed the wall. As we worked on through the summer and into the fall, it seemed to me sometimes that we were paving the road with our own bones, that the stones themselves were only a façade.

She found me in early August. Charles McLaughlin saw her first, and rather than alerting me he let me keep on working, hammering the sledge into the dry riverbed. He set about sketching her as she approached, and it was not until he had finished drawing her and closed his sketchbook and tugged on my chain that I looked up and saw her.

She had cut her hair short for the summer, and was wearing a long white cotton dress and leather sandals, and she was smiling to see me. She greeted Charles McLaughlin and then stepped up and touched my arm lightly before saying anything. She stepped back and looked at McLaughlin again.

McLaughlin cleared his throat and turned away, walked off to the full reach of the chain like a dog at the end of its tether, and when the chain reached full stretch, she saw me wince, with my own ankles chafed, old calluses worn back to raw skin in the drier heat of August.

I asked McLaughlin to help me position a link of the chain on a flat rock, and then lifted the sledge up and brought the point of it down hard, snapping the link and cleaving the chain into rattling halves.

The feeling of freedom was so profound that both Charles McLaughlin and I laughed — the chains felt as light as a kite string — and I took her hand and broke into a run, still laughing.

We ran upriver, picking our way around loose stones, and

around the bend, out of sight, where, sweating and breathless, we found a driftwood log on which to sit.

She said she had heard that a small stone house had been built near where we had met before.

"That was a surprise," I said, "for you. *Lo has visto?*"

"*No la he visto,*" she said. "*He escuchado que fue muy linda.*"

Even with my pidgin Spanish I thought I noticed the use of the past tense, but I decided it was simply some aspect of the language I had not yet learned.

"I would like for us to go there," I said. We were directly in the sun, with no shade at all — the driftwood log warm beneath us and the August sunlight giving parts of her hair that almost purple sheen — and now with a mixture of sadness and pleasure she said quietly, "*Me gusta.*"

"What do you think of the road?" I asked. "*El camino, la calle?*"

"*Es muy bonita,*" she said. "*He tocado las piedras frequentamente.*"

I pictured her doing that, walking on the road alone or with her friends, after we prisoners had been taken back to the garrison. Studying the slender red and green veins that ran through the otherwise all-white road like threads. Crouching and touching certain of them, knowing that I had touched them weeks and days earlier or, at the end of the road, perhaps only hours earlier. Noting the piles of rocks remaining stacked on the side of the road and the distance yet to travel: the time remaining before either I and the others would be sent to the Castle of Perve, in Perote, or — as we continued to hope — we might all be set finally free, because of the grudging success of our work on the road.

"*Mi padre —*" she began. "*Mi padre,*" she said again.

"*Yo sé ahora porque Bustamente no me deja ir a las piedras rojas,*" I said. "He found out I had been working on the *casita* there. But we could meet here at the green rocks." I looked around at the materials on hand: an endless supply of stones. "I can build a new *casita,* here," I said, gesturing to a shady bower. "Or I can slip out of the fort for a while. I can go over the wall," I said, "but Colonel Bustamente said that if there's one more escape, he'll be court-martialed, or maybe worse."

The color left her face, and she sat back and looked at me. "*Repitalo de nuevo,*" she said.

I tried to say it in Spanish. "*No hay que ser mas escapadas.* No more mistakes. Colonel Bustamente has told us he is on —" I searched for the word — "*probación.*" If there is any more trouble, he will lose his job, and" — I shrugged — "maybe his life."

She lowered her head, and I took her hands again and said, "*Que pasa? Que pasa?*"

Upstream, we heard the sound of the iron sledge beginning again. Charles McLaughlin, the artist, was trying to buy us time with the sound of his rock-smashing. Anyone would be able to tell that there was something totally different about the cadence and force, or lack of it, with which he was striking the rocks — if anything, it seemed to me it would arouse more suspicion than assurance — but it was a kind gesture, and I smiled.

"*Mi padre es Bustamente,*" Clara said flatly, watching me to see that I understood. And for a moment, I did not. I heard what she was saying but did not want to believe that she was speaking literally — preferring that she meant that he was like a father, or that he knew her father, or that he might even be related to her father.

"*No es importante,*" I said, reaching for her, but she shook her head and said, "Yes, it is important. *Para mi, para ti, para el.*" She shrugged helplessly and said, almost in a whisper, "*Sí, es importante.*"

The sledging had stopped again and there was only river-sound and the silence of the day, and the heat. "Does he know?" I asked.

"Does he know what?" She shook her head sadly. "*No hay nada que saber. Una pequeña casa, nada mas.*"

Over her shoulder, I saw now that the real reason Charles McLaughlin had started sledging was to warn me that two guards had come down to the river. I saw them advancing toward us, rifles in hand. I looked down at the broken chain still attached to my ankle: the half-length of it looking like a dead snake.

"*El sabe,*" Clara said. Another lift of her shoulders. "*Lo ha prohibido.*"

The soldiers were coming closer and were walking more quickly. She heard a stone clatter under their feet, and she turned, making a small sound, and stood abruptly. I rose too, and they looked roughly at her and then pushed me with the tips of their rifles, shoving me in the direction from which they had come. They said not a single word but took me back to my quarry, poking me with the ends of their rifles from time to time, with Clara trailing a short distance behind us, looking grief stricken, and the broken chain dragging and slithering over the rocks.

*　　*　　*

153

Unwilling to abandon me, Charles McLaughlin was waiting by the rock pile, his face bruised. "I told them you went the other direction," he said, "but they knew I was lying."

It was only when I saw Charles McLaughlin's battered face that it occurred to me that they might kill us, or that Bustamente might execute us. They led us up the trail, not bothering to reattach our chains — and at the top of the bluff, the guard informed Clara that he had been told to escort her back to town, while the other guard was to take us back to the road.

"You will not see her again, *muchacho*," her guard said, as the other guard prodded McLaughlin and me with his rifle. I looked back at her but her guard stepped between her sight and mine, and our guard shoved me around and marched us down the new shining road.

Bustamente did not execute us, but he put us back to work on the road, bound in new chains, and I was not allowed to quarry stones anymore; neither was Charles McLaughlin allowed to sketch. The red thread in the road had ended, as had the green thread, so similar in design to the little shoots and suckers that regenerated from the river-swept cottonwoods, and the fronds that had shaded the little stone house, never used.

"Aye, soldados desgraciados" was the only greeting we received upon returning to the road, our new chains a source of curiosity to our fellow prisoners. No one ever knew: only Charles McLaughlin and I.

In late August, Fisher and twelve other men began to make plans to escape on the twenty-first of September — the night before the grand ceremony that would celebrate the road's completion. For three weeks, I held that secret as I worked beneath Bustamente's gaze, laying down one heavy paving stone after another, condemning him to death with each day of my silence. I remembered Clara, there on the log, and thought about how it would be if she lost him.

I kept hoping the plan would collapse so that I would not have to act, but when, ten days before the celebration, I saw that Fisher and the others had knotted their sheets, I wrote a note to Bustamente, telling him only that sheets were missing and some of the prisoners were acting strange. I wrote it in Spanish, and though I wanted to sign my name in an attempt to win his favor, and perhaps win Clara, I could not bring myself to do it. I left the note lying in the road and watched while a guard wandered over, picked it up, and read it, frowning, then took it over to Bustamente.

When the colonel had finished reading it, he lifted his head and looked directly at me — I looked back down at the road, quickly — and I blushed, and wondered if he suspected me. It made perfect sense: I had betrayed him once. Why would I not betray also my fellow *soldados*?

He posted extra guards within the garrison at night and curtailed all town privileges, so that Fisher, cursing, was forced to cancel the escape attempt.

By late September, we were finished. Our own work — the final stretch of Tacubaya Road, six years in the building — had taken more than five months. A grand celebration was planned on the equinox to commemorate the opening. The leaves of the ash and sycamore trees were a beautiful gold color, and many had fallen from the trees and lined the sides of the road. We had swept the road free of all grit and rubble so that it was gleaming in the autumn light, and we were proud of our work, dazzled by its beauty.

Santa Anna himself would not be attending as we had hoped, but his personal secretary was traveling to Molino del Rey to participate, and we continued to hope that he would be so awed by our work that our sentences — eternal prisoners of war — would be remanded and we could return to our country.

Santa Anna's secretary spent a good bit of time with Captains Green and Fisher that evening, and before departing the next day he ordered that our chains be removed — but in the end, that was the only dispensation we received for all our work. Three days later we received the news that, with our work on the Tacubaya Road completed, we were to resume our march toward the Castle of Perve.

6

THE CASTLE OF PERVE

DESPITE OUR DESPAIR over failing to be released, the forced march to Perote felt like freedom compared to the fortress at Molino del Rey. We left the valley floor and went up into the mountains, which during the rainy season were usually swathed in clouds. We smelled the fresh sweet scent of fir and pine and saw tropical ferns and the late-season bloomings of tens of thousands of orchids. There were bromeliads — Charles McLaughlin had read about them, and told us about them excitedly — plants with upturned spiny leaves that formed cups and goblets holding so much rainwater that sometimes they supported little populations of minnows, which in turn fed on the mosquito larvae living in those same cupped flower goblets. Each blossom was its own tiny world, with the world's struggles within, and as McLaughlin pointed them out, nearly all two hundred of us, Mexicans and Texans alike, crowded around him to listen and to take turns peering into the flower.

Transfixed, we each crouched beside it, staring into its shallow waters as if into a wishing well, watching the translucent little fish hanging suspended in their horizontal positions, finning steadily, and the wriggling little commas of wiggletails on the surface. Columns of sunlight came down through the treetops and illuminated the depths of the tiny world into which we were staring like giants.

Still fascinated, we began to wander off in groups of a dozen or more, looking for more bromeliads, the guards strangely indulging us, as if they too had fallen under the forest's spell. Finding more, we would stare again in rapture, until it was only with great difficulty and some reluctance themselves that our captors were able to urge us on: and we departed wistfully, passing down off the mountain, with the sparkling drops of the last night's rain still dripping from the canopy, and we kept looking all around for more bromeliads, our sandals squishing at every step.

Our clothes were drenched, and when the sun was filtering down through the canopy our backs and shoulders steamed in that gold light, as did the necks and backs of the horses and mules.

Where once we had sweltered and burned in the desert, we now rotted. At first our feet merely itched, but then the flesh grew tattered and bloody, until it seemed our feet could no longer support us. We cut tree limbs to use as crutches, and in the steady rain we moved through a bright green paradise of creatures we had never seen before, long-billed toucans and parakeets. Sorrow-faced monkeys followed us, clicking their teeth and conferring among one another, as if empathizing with the misfortune that had brought us so far from home. Such was our misery that guard and captive were prisoners alike, merging as if back to a single army. One day Shields Booker asked to borrow a gun from a guard and then turned and fired at one of the monkeys that was following us in the falling rain. The bullet struck the monkey in the chest, and he fell backward, clutching the wound; and rather than fleeing, the rest of the band hurried to him and gathered around their fallen comrade, tending to him as he died.

We followed ancient stone-lined trails through the mountains, covering in our ceaseless, limping procession more than twenty miles a day. After only a week we had given up any efforts to stay dry, and when darkness fell each day we merely curled up in the mud and mulch beneath the dripping fronds of giant ferns and slept amid the hissing rain.

I dreamt often of being in a river, riding it downcurrent. Many of the men developed rattling coughs and chills, and we buried several along the trail. We no longer even said words at their burying but simply carved out a trough in the stony soil as best as we could and laid them into it, the trough filling with water even as we did so, and then covered them back up and resumed our march. I thought of Clara and felt utterly that my life had become a failure in every way.

After another two hundred miles — nearly nine hundred miles from home, now — we reached the pass into the valley and village of Perote, seven thousand feet above sea level. Other mountains, mist-shrouded volcanic spires and crags, towered nearly twice as high above us — the Cofre de Perote, and others, many of them capped with snow and ice — and it was a humbling experience to pass beneath them.

We passed down out of the rainy mountains — the stripe-faced monkeys continued to follow us for a while, as if they too were our captors, and parakeets flew back and forth, blazes of emerald and gold and crimson, while brightly colored butterflies rose from the tangle of ferns and flowers with swarming, fluttering beauty — and then the castle appeared before us, perched at the edge of the mountains, with the barren, shimmering sprawl of ash-gray volcanic plains stretching far below, all the way to the coast at Vera Cruz.

A slashing purple rain was hurling itself against the prison, and black clouds were stacked up to the horizon, awaiting their turn to drift across the castle before continuing on out into the desert, where they would dissipate without dropping any water on the boneyard plains below — evaporating in midair above that dazzling playa — and though a sodden chill ran through each of us as we saw where we were to be housed perhaps for the rest of our mortal days, we could not help but also feel awe at the utter defensibility of the fort.

It had literally been carved into the mountain. The jutting neck of an old volcano had been cut out, countless buckets of rubble and slag hammered and hauled away by Indian slaves, across the centuries — and scattered across the blackened mountain, where basalt had been forged and cast by the earth's original fire and then cooled beneath the breath of the world, were other parapets and turrets, the remnants of smaller volcano necks in which soldiers could take refuge and fire upon any approaching armies.

So perfectly did the fort blend into the rainy black mountain that at first glance I didn't even see it. Once I had detected its subtle pattern against the mountains, a kind of horror grew as I realized the size and extent of it — that the entire mountain face was a fortress and prison.

As we approached, we saw that cannons protruded from every embrasure. Our captors raised the flag of Mexico and called out, and in a driving rain we crossed a moat twenty feet deep and fifty feet wide, and entered the gates, which were made of giant cedar logs and were defended by countless high parapets with guns and cannons protruding in all directions. The stone walls themselves were sixty feet high, and, looking up, it seemed to us that there was an entire nation of soldiers atop those walls, all of them peering down at us as we had earlier gazed down at the tiny creatures living in the water-filled cups of the orchids.

The water in the moat was sparkling clear. Lily pads, their blossoms alternately butter yellow and snow white, floated in the crystal waters, and white swans paddled back and forth, elegant and yet strangely military-looking. We studied them hungrily and imagined how good they would taste. Bigfoot Wallace tossed a rock at the swans and one of the larger drakes responded with a high squeal. Wallace warned us that the swans were sentinels and would sound an alarm if we tried to escape.

The first thing we saw upon entering the prison — other than the legions of guards assigned to defend it, and to stand watch over all the other prisoners already assembled there, generations of military and political prisoners — was a torrent of clear sparkling water gushing from the roaring wide mouth of a stone-carved lion. Channels had been carved and dug so water could run beneath the fort in underground aqueducts, and, looking back out at the windy pumice desert, just before the gates closed for good, we saw now that there were numerous such lions and bears and gargoyles carved into the cliff's walls, their fierce mouths and once sharp fangs polished from where water had coursed in the past. We understood that, besides serving as a barrier, the water could also be used as a weapon: certain underground flows could be adjusted and transferred to cause great torrents of water to begin spouting from the mouths of the animals, making it more difficult for an attacking enemy to scale the walls.

The immense, uninhabited mountains towering above us — the snowfields and glaciers — yielded a steady and perhaps limitless supply of clean water to the fort, water that passed through those engineered channels and reservoirs before draining back underground and beneath us, audible through the porous rock in those secret aqueducts. Hearing it splash and splatter out into the moat beyond, I was reminded of the strange dream that young John Alexander had had up in the Sierra de la Paila mountains following our flights from Salado, back when we had been dying of thirst.

Our first act in the prison at Perote, in the Castle of Perve, was to kneel around the plunge pool beneath the mouth of the lion and drink like cattle from those clear waters, with the sound of the heavy gate being closed and latched tight behind us.

We had imagined we might be housed in separate cells, so we were surprised and relieved to discover that we would all be herded into one long common room. Our captors led us down an ever-darkening hallway, past the heavy oaken doors of other such rooms in which the prisoners from other nations and even from Mexico herself were housed; and as we passed by each door, the inhabitants within, as if by some divine intuition, were able to discern our passage, and though they knew nothing of who we were or how we had come to be here, they each set up a howling and banging clamor, a blind and unknowing welcome.

We descended a flight of stone steps, as cold and dark and dank as would be our room itself, and stopped at a doorway, where there was a lectern with a cracked leather-bound journal atop it, a registry of all the prisoners who had occupied, for whatever periods of time, this one particular room in Perote across the centuries. As Charles McLaughlin thumbed through it, he stopped at one entry from only a few years earlier, September 1839, and read, "The walls of our dungeon are smoke-stained black and brown. The limestone plaster is still visible in only a few places. White saltpeter, which forms everywhere, is the only adornment of our damp abode. Spreading along the cracks in the walls and ceiling, it solidifies into formations of various shapes. With a little imagination one can see animals, human profiles, Saturn's rings, the Milky Way, the isthmus of Panama, and other things. The floor, half brick and half limestone mortar, is full of holes and not too easy to walk on. In one corner . . . there is a barrel; one can easily guess its purpose without my describing it. In the opposite corner there is another barrel that contains water, our daily beverage. On wooden pegs, protruding rocks, or on cords we hang our clothes, tools, and other things."

McLaughlin finished reading, and we filed into the room he had just described. We were relieved immediately by the relative spaciousness after the claustrophobia of the dark and narrow hall. The body heat from the mass of us attended our movements like a thunderstorm, a rank humidity that occupied any space we entered, and here, too, it followed us, emanated from us, and I remembered briefly the hope, the joy I had known down at the river, working on Bustamente's road, and then that memory passed, all but useless, from my mind.

In our long room there were high arches overhead. We could sense that we were in the maw of the earth, below ground, to the depth of that one flight of stairs, but high above our heads at the far end of the room there was a single grate through which one lean trapezoid of light entered from the world above.

We began staking out our individual cots, with Green and Fisher and Wallace and their aides securing the prime beds, closest to that little wedge of light that would never quite reach the floor of our dungeon.

I had thought Charles McLaughlin would seek out some private place where he could practice his craft in the evenings, undisturbed by the nightly card games and songs and dances — but he dragged a bed into the center of the dungeon and positioned it just so beneath that slightly angled, nearly flat trajectory of dying light — and I found myself following him, grabbing my own cot and sledding it into the center of the barracks also, rather than heading over to one of the corners, as had been my initial inclination.

We walked out into the courtyard and stood in line for our food, and were astonished to see one of the guards aim his musket at his commanding officer. We were to learn later that they had been quarreling for months.

The officer ducked just as the musket discharged, and the bullet struck one of our young irregulars, Shields Booker, in the neck. The prison medics did all they could for him, but he died twenty-four hours later and was buried in the moat (only Catholics were allowed to be buried in the prison cemetery), in a service made all the more poignant in that it was attended by the silent swans, who gathered around the ripples left by Booker's stone-weighted coffin after it had slipped straight to the bottom.

At the moatside funeral service, I looked over at Charles McLaughlin, who was, as ever, sketching vigorously, and I tried to look at the scene around me, and the world, the way he might be seeing it: not what it had been moments before Booker had been shot, and not what it might be after the funeral, but what it was *now*, as if that were all it ever would be; and then on to the next sketch, and the next.

It was tempting to look at the world that way — without fear — but it still seemed important to me, more than ever, not to delude myself, but to remember that the world was a dangerous place.

Charles McLaughlin lifted his head briefly from his agitated scratchings and looked over at me for a moment — I thought he was contemplating drawing me, and, knowing that if he did the fright on my face would be revealed, I turned away.

Breakfast each day consisted of a tiny bowl of cornmeal gruel sweetened with brown sugar, and a single cup of coffee: hardly enough for the tasks demanded of us, which included carpentry, latrine duties, more road-building, cleaning the stables, and, once again, quarrying stones for other construction projects.

Lunch was no better. Jittery-legged with fatigue, we would crowd around a cauldron of simmering water into which had been tossed an onion or two, a handful of salt and rice, some red peppers, and occasionally the offal of a cow or horse or pig — bones, hoofs, hide, entrails, brains, and whatever else the guards would not eat.

Back to work we would be sent, then, dysenteric and choleric, with dinner that evening consisting once more of gruel. Only occasionally were we given the opportunity to use our meager earnings to purchase a piece of fruit — a banana, or sometimes a single red strawberry.

Fisher and Green appeared to be reversing roles.

Green, previously the fierce patriot and lover of the land, seemed to be losing his interest in the revolution, despairing at the threat to our new nation's independence, as well as the loss of his own. Once in the Castle of Perve, the two officers no longer received the special courtesies that had been extended to them before and were instead forced to work alongside the rest of us, rotating through the same insufferable and demeaning tasks and duties of captivity.

And while such menial and humbling labor seemed to be having a positive effect on Fisher, making him more human, and more accessible to us, Green now seemed estranged and haunted, collapsing into himself, sinking like a dense stone dropped into a dark, slowing river.

Green was spending increasing amounts of time alone in

the evenings, penning angry letters back to Sam Houston in Texas, and to the United States government, and to Santa Anna, alternately threatening, cajoling, pleading, bargaining, and haranguing, working at the far end of the dungeon by that gridwork opening through which a few dim stars could be seen, and sometimes, briefly, the clockwork gear passage of the moon in its revolution around us — while the rest of us, Fisher included, entertained ourselves at night in the center of our cell with dances and skits and songs and games.

Not Green, however. He burned bitterly, stewing in the toxins of injustice. Petty things were consuming him now, final tiny straws upon the long-suffering camel's back. At the Battle of San Jacinto, years earlier, following Santa Anna's surrender to Houston, Green had given General Houston his fine, new, unbloodied officer's coat to help keep an exhausted Santa Anna warm against the April chill. In gratitude, Santa Anna had given General Houston a jeweled snuffbox, which Green, eyeing it covetously, had valued at being worth about a thousand dollars.

Being a junior officer then, Green had received nothing from the transaction, and now, seven years later, in his letters to both Houston and Santa Anna, he badgered them about this, trying somehow to parlay this inequity into his own personal freedom at least, if not that of his men. He informed Santa Anna that he had once defended Santa Anna's honor by reprimanding a soldier who said something unflattering about the Mexican leader; surely this favor deserved some reciprocal notice.

In the jail cell, in addition to having ample opportunity to blacken the pages of various ledgers and journals with the accounts of our imprisonment and to pen letters home (in which we tried not to let anyone know how squalid and dire conditions truly were), we had access occasionally to old newspapers, some of them many months out of date, from the Republic of Texas, as well as the United States — Memphis and New Orleans, mostly. We all knew that both Houston and Santa Anna were in political trouble over matters far more immediate and pressing than our imprisonment — that Mexico was hugely in debt and could not much longer afford to field an army without the financial assistance of Great Britain, and that the United States, desiring to annex Texas, was afraid that Great Britain might be trying to take control.

In essence, Sam Houston's new nation — our new nation — was simultaneously under siege from at least six other nations — three at once, in a loose coalition of Apaches, Comanches, and Kiowas; Mexico; Great Britain, which wanted to either control Texas or at least keep Texas out of the United States' hands; and the United States itself, which desired to peacefully absorb our new nation (even as, twenty years later, they would wage war against us — deservedly so — over the issue of human slavery).

We should never have crossed that river. What madness could possibly have possessed us?

Centuries' worth of vermin inhabited every crack and crevice of the dank fort. They did not even wait until true dark to emerge but began scuttling out well before dusk and did not return to their burrows until long after dawn's first light. Rats, mice, scorpions, dung beetles, and roaches whirred and raced and scrabbled everywhere, bumping into us if we should get in their way, outnumbering us by the thousands. They stank and shat and pissed and gnawed incessantly on the wooden legs of furniture, and on one another's bones. They fought and squealed and snarled and chattered, some of the rats as large as cats, though fiercer; but worst of all were the lice, which could hide anywhere, and which, though silent, seemed to be born of the night, with the ranks of each night's army swelling tenfold.

They awakened us every evening, pouring out from between the weave of our blankets and from our hair, and from the fur of all the living mammals in the fort. They began swarming us almost the minute we fell asleep, so many of them moving across the stone floor that in the near darkness of soft moonlight it appeared that the floor itself was moving, with waves and ripples of the milky white crablike creatures rolling across the floor like the phosphorescent foam of waves at sea. We would turn and rattle our blankets every few moments, trying to shake them off, but always they returned, drawn relentlessly by the heat of our bodies and by the bright blood within us. To defend against them we shaved our heads and grew our fingernails long so that we could pluck them from each other's bodies.

In the evenings we would hold louse races, using charcoal to draw a circle in the center of the dungeon, placing lice in the center, and then wagering on which one would reach the perimeter the soonest. We had little money so gambled instead with fragments of soap, called *tlacos*, or used and reused remnants of tobacco, gotten from the stubs of pipes and cigarettes, chewed and then dried to use again and again.

With livestock in poor condition and short supply at the

fort, we ourselves were often forced into service, fitted with rawhide harnesses, twenty-five men to a team, and made to pull oxcarts filled with stones down out of the mountains. The road was steep, and sometimes we lost control by accident, though other times it was on purpose. We would slip out of our harnesses and watch as the runaway wagon, with its heavy load, went thundering down the hill before crashing into a wall or into the moat, upsetting the swans.

We devised new ways to get rid of our chains. The most common trick was to smash one link with a stone, then go to the blacksmith who, for the bribe of a few cents, would replace the old iron rivet with a softer and more malleable lead one. We could then remove the chains at will while the guards were gone and then fasten them back together when the guards returned.

We called the chains our "jewelry," and often, late at night after the final lockup and roll call, we would all one hundred and fifty be shed of our chains and would sleep, even if fitfully, among the lice and rats in relative freedom: though the morning's first dull shaft of light and the sound of the guards stirring outside would send us all scrambling to put the chains back on.

In the Castle of Perve, there were no positive incentives to do good work or behave. When we were discovered free of our chains, or when we broke an oxcart or failed to move a satisfactory amount of stone in a day, we were punished; our only reward was no punishment.

Beatings were infrequent — as if they might be too burdensome for our captors to inflict upon our thick skulls and hides — but far more common were trips to the *calabozo*, a tiny closet of solitary confinement, for days on end, after which the old captivity seemed by comparison the sweetest of freedoms.

Less stern measures included attaching heavy iron or wooden crossbars between our ankle chains, which caused us to trip and stumble all day, or, on Sundays, fastening a gigantic cross to a prisoner's back and making him haul it far up the mountain, with the guards and townspeople of Perote being able to glance up at that giant cross moving up the mountain, at any time of day, and gauge the slow ascent as if it were but one more louse race.

Our captors were particularly fond of forcing Bigfoot Wallace to carry a cross — fashioning an improbably oversized one for him to haul — and it never ceased to amaze me how, despite the punishment, they were unable to break his spirit. Some of the larger crosses took him three days and nights to get to the top, but he never complained, and told us afterward that compared to our time in the *calabozo*, such trips were almost like freedom itself, or what we remembered of freedom.

Some two thousand feet above the fort there was a rough volcanic ridge lined with scores of giant crosses, the spoor of recalcitrant prisoners from the past. After laboring all day without food or water — sometimes in an icy, rattling, sheet-driven wind, other times beneath a broiling sun — the prisoner had to erect the mammoth cross on that ridge and pile stones around the base to keep it from blowing over. (If the cross did blow over, the prisoner was required to go up there, drag it all the way back down the mountain, and then start over again the next day.)

Over the years, however, crosses had fallen, so that there were as many lying on the ground as there were standing, and there were crosses leaning halfway between sky and ground, so that spars and beams silhouetted the ridge in a myriad of angles, looking like a buck-and-rail fence. It was a tangle of dissymmetry, with some of the more ancient crosses beginning to crumble and rot on the stony ledge, while others still exuded the green odor of heavy new-sawn wood, and still others bore the stains from our bloodied and blistered backs, as we ourselves still bore splinters from that engagement. There was none among us who had not hauled at least one cross to the ridge, and such punishment did not dispose us favorably toward the Catholic race.

The U.S. ambassador, Waddy Thompson, was soon to become a staunch friend and ally, our one crux of support from the outside. Whenever he came to visit us, brimming with an encouraging mix of optimism and forcefulness, we felt hopeful, and whenever he left or was out of touch with us for too long — a month, two months, three months — we felt abandoned, rejected, even betrayed, and consumed by a fever of fear and loneliness and the damnable longing for freedom.

Each time Waddy Thompson reappeared — a gentleman, a man of power — our hearts leapt, and each time he left while we remained, we began again the long trek back down into misery and servitude, until in some ways it seemed that we were as much his prisoners as we were the Mexican government's, despite our knowing better.

We could never have wished for a better ally. He devoted more time to us than his job called for. It simply wasn't enough. Our needs were bottomless. No one man, and perhaps no nation, or nations, could extricate us; neither could we ourselves. We were captive to all who looked upon us, prisoners even to our own hearts, for we had not merely "lost" our freedom but willfully given it up, back when we had first crossed the border at Fisher's strident urging.

As ever, McLaughlin sketched in the evenings, choosing to spend his precious coins not on lead rivets or fruit or illicit mouthfuls of mescal passed from guard to prisoner, but on candles, so that he might work far into the night. When he ran out of pencils he used the smudge of charcoal, so that his hands and face were soon almost always smeared black. I would sit up with him often, reading or occasionally writing letters to those back home. And from the way he sketched, throwing himself into it with such unnerving focus, I wondered often if he even understood any longer that he was still a prisoner: there was something that made me think he did not, and I was envious.

Escape was no longer on our minds; we were broken, hobbled. In a general letter to his many friends back in Texas, R. A. Barclay wrote, "When we shall guet out of this snap God only knows. My only hope is an exchange of prisners . . . things growes daily more gloomey . . . they treat us worse evry day. The Mexicans point me out and say I am the worst one in the Castle — I have worn hobels two weeks, binn beat with there spades and muskets, calaboosed and evry means to cow me they can think of . . . There is no hope of release."

Peter Maxwell, in a letter addressed to various newspapers, designed to sway the sympathies of Sam Houston, complained, "Our overseers . . . often beat we Texians with sticks with as little ceremony as we would beat Negroes." And in an official complaint to Waddy Thompson — who on his last visit had said not to despair, that he was still working to somehow gain our release — Fenton Gibson, not a true Texan but a Kentuckian, and a grandson of Daniel Boone, wrote, "What then must be the deep agony of an American to be struck by one of these imps of darkness . . .? Sir, it is insupportable. The blood on an American cannot brook the degradation."

In a letter to his wife, Norman Woods lied, trying to assuage her fears, and spoke proudly of the heroic regularity of his bowels. "We have plenty to eat, good clothes to wear, fine coffee to drink twice a day, meat once, good flour bread with three kinds of cracked seeds in it. I am coopering and make about one bucket a week."

Beneath that dark mountain, haunted by the sound of the fresh water rushing through the labyrinth of aqueducts just beneath us night and day, and under such steady oppression, our old dreams and fevers unraveled and ran wandering in a hundred and forty different directions, as if seeking to trickle back down into the stony soil beneath us.

Beneath our crosses and hobbles, and beneath the beatings and the lice, we continued to fall further, until we finally reached the bottom, at which point it was every man for himself: and sometimes not even that.

One by one, like the occasional sparrows that would find their way into our dungeon through the grate, flutter confused for a while, and then find their way back out, a few of our number were plucked from the group and turned free, by the deux ex machina we had all been dreaming of back before our spirits began to break. Two prisoners were released when the U.S. president, Andrew Jackson, sent Santa Anna a special letter asking for their release. Years earlier, following the surrender at San Jacinto, when Santa Anna had been so despondent he had attempted suicide, Jackson had invited Santa Anna to visit the United States, where he had been treated with dignity and respect, at a time when his own government, shamed by his defeat, wanted nothing to do with him.

Soon a third prisoner, George B. Crittenden, was also released — he was the son of the Kentucky senator John Crittenden, who, being a Whig, was an enemy of Jackson's but a colleague nonetheless.

These strange mercies began stirring, once again, the still-warm ashes of hope in our souls.

Some, alas, responded without valor. A prisoner from San Antonio, Judge James W. Robinson, who had served briefly as lieutenant governor of Texas in the months preceding the Alamo, began crafting a complex plan of compromise in which the Republic of Texas could be induced to return to Mexico's rule in exchange for some assurance of limited autonomy. Robinson proposed that he himself should be the mediator in such convoluted bargaining, which would of course necessitate his being released from the Castle of Perve.

His gambit worked. Santa Anna fell for it, and soon Robinson was back in Texas, having gained an audience with Sam Houston at Washington-on-the-Brazos.

Texas's newspapers went berserk upon hearing the proposal — "The blood of the patriots who had secured our hard-fought independence barely yet dry," they cried — but nonetheless, Robinson's proposal, though ludicrous on its face, did connect with a larger underlying sentiment that craved stability in the aftermath of so much war.

The new nation hungered also for the prosperity that peace could bring, and from Robinson's half-baked idea discussion of another kind of peace-making — an armistice — began to develop. Again, the annexation discussions were resurrected. *Who would get Texas, and at what price, and under what terms?*

Out of Robinson's trickery a flickering peace seemed to be emerging. Perhaps it was just a good year for peace, as certain years are occasionally favorable for some rare crop; whatever the reason, Sam Houston — whose first son was born that spring — was ebullient, and began pursuing the armistice with Mexico with new vigor. To his friend Ashbel Smith he wrote, "The new nation could no longer afford the expense of war, and the idea of the Armistice has cheered our people, and the vicious, traitorous and factious are confounded." And with hope rising, he wrote, "Our Mexican relations have assumed a more promising aspect. Let us never despair of the Republic; but like true citizens obey the laws, love order, be industrious, live economically, and all will soon be well. Noisy, non-productive and disappointed men, who hate labor and aspire to live upon the people's substance, have already done us great injury abroad. At home they are too well known to be any longer feared."

Charles McLaughlin kept sketching. Hundreds of pages now filled his portfolio. There were portraits decorating the dark stone walls of our cell and lining the walls of the prison outside the cell, stuck to the stone with dried gruel. Even the guards and soldiers were posting his works in their quarters and occasionally giving him a few pesos for them, which he used not for whiskey or tobacco or even extra food but to buy new art supplies.

Waddy Thompson was becoming increasingly enamored with Mexico — he had not been back to his home in South Carolina in years. He was too comfortable, some of the prisoners groused, calling him "Mexicanized," alarmed by the way he seemed more and more to be speaking in the Spanish tongue rather than English, though he continued to assure us that he was working diligently for our release. Green complained, "I think now he is a good hand at 'Wind Work' only."

Green would have been even further enraged if he had known what we were all to learn later, which was that to increase his chances for successful diplomacy, Thompson was secretly pocketing some of our less tactful letters back home, as well as our letters to Jackson, Houston, and Santa Anna — including several of Green's invective-filled rhetorical howls.

Still, we could have wished for no finer ally. As U.S. ambassador, it was not even his job to represent us — we were still a separate nation — but he jokingly referred to himself as the Patron Saint of Lost Causes.

At night, while Charles McLaughlin sketched by candlelight, with a halo of sputtering moths circling his flame and casting wild shadows against the stone walls, and surrounded by the snoring and gurgling, hacking coughs of our fellow prisoners, I would think about the men I might have killed so long ago, back in Mier; and of the wrongful foundation of our expedition, the faulty first step, our pillage back in

Laredo — back on our own free soil, no less. I would be seized with a kind of despair, a dejected acceptance of our fate, knowing that we deserved the misery that had befallen us and that even our captivity was a kind of blessing or mercy in that we were fortunate to at least have had our lives spared.

I would stand beneath the lone grate, looking up at three or four dim stars. I could hear as ever the rush of unseen river below, flowing through and beneath the mountain, louder and so much clearer at night, and if I strained I could hear sounds from much farther away, the breeze that seemed to bathe those stars, polishing them and making them glimmer. From just beyond the fort came the muted gabblings of the swans, and the sound of the wind lapping little waves against the moat's walls.

I knew that at night nearly all the animals in the desert came from miles away to drink from the moat — on our stone-load oxcart trips the next day, or our cross-hauling punishments, I had seen the stipplings of their tracks in the dust, prints of deer, antelope, bobcat, bear, javelina, jaguar, raccoon, skunk, fox, and panther — and it seemed to me as I stood there at the grate that I could hear them splashing and bathing in the moat's waters.

It seemed too that I could hear the night-mutter of red-winged blackbirds, rustling with reeds as they were disturbed briefly by the larger-bodied slither of deer and antelope into those waters, the splashing of the lions and jaguars and the wolves and coyotes, the night-trilling of frogs.

Green was cracking. He had taken to blaming us for his captivity — arguing, yet again, that we should have fought harder at Mier, should never have surrendered. His father, still on the Tennessee Supreme Court, had sent word that he had failed now in his entreaties for his son's clemency to not one but two presidents — first Jackson, then Tyler. Green's own letters, alternately ranting and cajoling, had gotten him nowhere, even as other prisoners, one by one, had been slipping through those iron grates.

Green began to circulate among us once more, interrupting our card games, trying to encourage others to make another escape attempt. He had several takers — most surprising of all ex-captain Reese, who had been so reluctant back at Salado, refusing to escape even when the gate had been opened.

All this time, Reese had been writing his own appeals, arguing that he should be rewarded for his moderation, but finally, seeing that he was receiving treatment no better than the rest of us, he too began to crack. "We are going to die here," he said. "We are going to rot here. We must do what we can — no one will save us." He agreed with Green that we had to make another attempt soon, and told us that many nights he dreamt that we were already dead and rotted, and that the dream was real, while all else — *"this,"* he said, pinching his wizened arm — was the dream.

"Are you going?" Charles McLaughlin asked me one night.

"I don't know," I said.

"Do you want to get out?" he asked.

"Of course," I said. "But . . ."

"But what?" he said. "Reese is right. We have to leave *now*."

We began digging, working at night. The prison walls were eight feet thick, but because much of the stone was volcanic pumice, it was fairly easy to chisel. Many of the men worked in the carpentry shop, building the frames and wagons for cannons and other heavy artillery weapons, so they had easy access to chisels and hammers.

Charles McLaughlin moved his bunk over to the wall where they were digging in order to be in a better position to illustrate the operation.

To dispose of the rubble, each of us carried a load to the latrines three times a day, whether we were in on the escape or not. The horizontal tunnel, about two feet wide, was hidden by a small boulder. If Bigfoot Wallace wanted to escape, he would have to dig his own, for it was calculated that a three-foot-wide tunnel would have taken twice as long.

Sixteen men were planning to escape. Each man would carry enough food for at least two weeks. We each began to purchase and hoard small amounts of bacon fat, chocolate, hardtack, sugar, and dried fruit, as well as anything that was packaged with rope or twine, which we then wove into one larger, stronger rope, for the prisoners to use in scaling the wall once they had passed through the tunnel.

Once the tunnel was finished, the plan called for us — for them — to wait for a rainy night, since the guards usually skipped the evening roll call, which took place in the courtyard, when it rained.

We waited for a week, trembling with anticipation — so much so that I worried the guards would hear the clamor of our hearts. I still didn't know if I would be going or not. If I got free, I had decided to head for Texas. It would be tempting to go find Clara again, but sheer folly, too, and I had had enough of folly.

Fisher refused to be part of the escape. He had been brooding over some of Green's accusations, and when the rain finally came, Fisher surprised us all by saying he would be remaining behind, vowing not to leave the Castle of Perve until every prisoner had been freed.

He and Green stood in front of the tunnel opening, briefly facing each other — they said nothing but shook hands stiffly, formally — and I had the impression that Fisher would have embraced Green but that Green would have none of it. Slipping out of their jewelry, the men wriggled into the tunnel one by one, as if being swallowed by the mountain itself: and I was astounded when Charles McLaughlin, who up until that point had still been sketching the goings-on, scene by scene, laid down his charcoal and tablet and stood up and followed the other prisoners into the hole, pausing at the entrance only long enough to motion for me to join him.

I hesitated, and he turned and crawled into the tunnel, and Fisher placed the stone back in place. I felt the strangest mix of emotions: a savage joy mingled with the most awful kind of loneliness.

We stood there, our numbers lessened by seventeen — and then Fisher looked down at a note that Green had left with him, and began to laugh.

We had assumed the note was some formal transfer of command, or perhaps the letter Sam Houston had penned so long ago, authorizing us to cross the border in the first place and to engage the enemy wherever we might find him.

Instead, it was a letter from Green to Santa Anna. "Dear Sir," Fisher read. "Since I have recently discovered that the climate of Perote is not suiting to my health, I think that I should, for the present, retire to one in Texas that is more congenial to my feelings."

There was half a moment's silence and then our cell swelled with the uproar of our laughter. The guards came running to investigate, and we quickly pretended to be engaged in a raucous cup-banging dance: and if our ranks appeared significantly diminished, it was not apparent to our captors, who peered in and saw only the whirling-dervish jigs and reels of scraggly captives who had been kept too long imprisoned. They peered in, then turned away; roll call could wait until morning.

I could hear the rain running off the clay tiles in steady sheets, could feel the dampness emanating from those stones. I could see nothing around me but the dimmest shadowcast of candles, and the dark walls, and I yearned for nothing more than the feel of sunlight on my bare skin, and the privilege of laboring in the dry warmth of day, with clean air filling my lungs.

With my head leaning against the stones, it took a while before I realized I was hearing something other than the steady rain outside. The escapees had passed all the way through the tunnel, but upon reaching the outermost exit — the final wall, which lay beyond our wall — they found that the exit hole was still too small, that they had underestimated, and they were having to chisel it wider, working deep into the night, racing against the morning.

I listened for two hours. I had just about decided to try to join them when there finally came a silence, and then I thought I heard a few faint voices — guards, or prisoners, murmuring as if from within the rocks — and then more silence.

Surely they had been captured; surely it would be folly for me to go with them now.

I waited a while longer, listening to the silence of the stones, and then, from a different direction, with the rain still coming down in torrents, I heard the faintest, briefest sound of what sounded like the swans' warning calls. It was short-lived, questionable — almost like a sound imagined, rather than real — and though I froze, listening for it again, and then went over to the grate where I might hear better, it did not come again.

Some of the prisoners did not get very far. In the coming days, the guards and recaptured prisoners would tell us how it went, the guards praising us for not having participated in the escape.

After squeezing through the fortress tunnel and using their rope to climb over the point-sharpened, rain-slick logs at the far end of the fort, and swimming the moat (disturbing not just the swans but all the other wild animals that were gathered there), the escapees had split into small groups and run off into the desert, with each lightning flash revealing them to be scattered farther and farther from the castle, and from one another.

One prisoner broke both arms when he fell over the other side of the wall and nearly drowned; Green rescued him, dragged him to shore, and then left him there to fend for himself. He spent the rest of the rainy night shivering, surrounded by a menagerie of animals, and in the morning he was recaptured and executed; we heard the firing squad.

Other prisoners were hunted down by the cavalry, one by one, and executed. Each day I feared that Charles McLaughlin would be among them — but after a week had passed with no new prisoners being brought in, alive or dead, I relaxed, and we learned some weeks later that Green and a few others had made it to freedom. They had made it safely all the way to Mexico City, where some American friends had hidden them for several days in Jalapa, in the home of a rich and elderly Mexican national who was hostile to Santa Anna's violent regime.

This distinguished gentleman entrusted Green and his associates to a gang of *ladrones,* bandits, who ferried the Texans through secret jungle trails down to Vera Cruz, where a Frenchman gave them safe harbor for a week while they waited for an American steamer to pass through.

When one did, they slipped down to the beach at night, climbed aboard — the ship was bound for New Orleans — and were three days at sea when a plague of yellow fever struck them. The illness quickly ran its way through the sailors and escapees alike, killing half outright and incapacitating almost all of the others. But they were able to navigate the big ship back to America, half crashing it in the mouth of the Mississippi, where Indians were waiting for them. Some of the men, Green included, escaped into the brush even as the Indians were setting fire to the steamer — in its hold were no small amount of munitions, which began to explode with what seemed an unending fusillade of smoke and flame and artillery fire — and it was not until September that Green, fevered and gaunt, made it back to Texas, where he was hailed as a patriot and intrepid hero of the

Revolution, in addition to the latest and now most persistent thorn in Sam Houston's side.

Green ran for office the very next month — arriving home twenty-four hours in advance of the deadline to file for candidacy — and was elected to the Texas House of Representatives: and though we were not to learn of these things until many months later, when we did we received each piece of news with joy at the exploits of our captain, our mad captain, and William Fisher, whenever he heard the latest, smiled quietly.

Waddy Thompson came to see us after the escape. Usually positive and upbeat, he seemed dejected on this visit, and we soon learned why.

"Santa Anna was just about to release you," he told us. "My entreaties had been working, as had Britain's and the United States'. He was *this* close," he told us, holding his thumb and finger up: a bean-sized distance, a pea-sized distance. He dropped his hands in exasperation. "You should have told me," he said to Fisher. "I could have at least counseled postponement."

Fisher looked away, saying nothing.

Thompson sighed. "Santa Anna's precise words now are that your souls will rot in hell before you ever leave the Castle of Perve." He shook his head dejectedly. "I won't give up," he said. There were those in Britain who wanted us free, and many in the United States, and even some in Texas, and if only we could endure, he would keep trying to arrange the political puzzle pieces that might allow us to one day walk out as free men.

He said that in the past Santa Anna's impulsiveness might have worked to our advantage — that as he had once been quick with a grudge, so too had he been quick to forgive — but that the once brilliant, mercurial military hero was disintegrating, isolated at his Vera Cruz estate, drinking too much and immersing himself in the violent sport of cockfighting. Thompson had assisted him on numerous occasions and had found the sport — if it could be called that, he said — repellent.

As to whether we should attempt another escape, he said that earlier he would have advised against it wholeheartedly, but he was no longer sure what he himself would do, were he in our situation — though he reminded us that if any of us attempted escape and were captured, we would surely be executed. No longer would we be afforded the relative grace of the *diezmo*.

And though our old tunnel had been discovered and sealed back up with stones and mortar, and though our rations had been cut in half and we had each been made to haul crosses up onto the mountain, and though we were strip-searched daily, we nonetheless began digging another system of tunnels, hiding this one in the stony earth beneath the tile flooring so that it would pass not through the walls but beneath them, tunneling straight down toward the hypnotic sound of the underground river. We planned this time to dig down into the aqueduct, paint ourselves with charcoal until we were as black as night, and ride in crude handcarved rafts made from the reassembly of our cots, also painted with charcoal, down that rushing stone-lined underground river, past whatever few guards might be lounging around the place where it exited from the mountain —

passing beneath the spouting mouths of those stone-carved lions at night, and riding, as if over a small waterfall, the rushing waters that crashed out into the moat, at which point we, too, would scatter out into the desert, following the night stars east to Vera Cruz.

The typhus hit us that fall. The first symptoms were like those of yellow fever — crushing headaches, alternating with chills and nausea and disorientation — and in our relentless portages of the heavy crosses up the steep mountainside beneath the blue October sky, we clung to the mountain, and our crosses, as if to keep from being pitched off a suddenly dizzying earth. We had to stop often, lying down and curling up in the thin sun like dried fetuses expelled from some dying creature.

We were accused of malingering, were whipped and forced to work harder, but our stumbling gait grew worse, and after the first man died a physician was allowed to visit us.

The diagnosis was "jail fever," caused by a lack of fresh air and sunlight, poor diet, and melancholia. We were allowed to move our cots and bunks out into the courtyard, to sleep beneath the stars, though still chained together. Even in our infirm state, we nearly swooned with pleasure at what had once been our birthright.

A few of us rallied briefly, but soon another wave of the illness hit, fiercer the second time around, and now the contagion leapt not just from prisoner to prisoner but to our guards, and from our guards to the surrounding town of Perote.

At the time it was not understood that the lice were carriers of the typhus — that it was in their feces, which entered our bloodstream through our scratching at our endless bedsores, and then was passed to the guards and on to the rest of the town through the tiny drops of saliva in our coughs.

The disease raged through the winter, killing half of our number and thousands of Mexicans, in results that were ironically far superior to any we might have achieved through battle.

Every day, all through that autumn and winter, several of us were hauled across the drawbridge over the moat in ox-carts — some dead, some dying — to be dropped off at the hospital or buried in the desert beyond. During that time, we had to stop work on our new tunnel, for none of us was strong enough. We could hear the river below but could not travel to it.

Bigfoot Wallace was given last rites, but he survived somehow, and proclaimed of his Mexican physician afterward that he was "one of the best-hearted men" he ever knew. But we also saw some of the guards, and indeed some of the physicians and nurses, taking the last coins from the pockets of men whose bodies were still warm.

Men who had once been comrades now argued even unto their deaths. One relatively healthy prisoner refused to give a dying partner the twelve cents he needed to buy a piece of fruit in his final hours. Others prowled among the dying, crafting last wills and testaments in which they would inherit the paltry possessions of the dead. Through it all, the lice continued to scuttle from the porous stones, and the winter rains beat down upon the baked-clay tile roofs, flooding the courtyard and turning the old castle into a choking, coughing, stinking quagmire. Those of us who continued to survive grew as gaunt as skeletons, and so hollow of dreams that we could barely remember our past lives.

We burned Charles McLaughlin's many hundreds of sketches for warmth, and often we wondered if those who died were not in a better place than those who survived. At the hospital we were lashed to cots so that we could not scratch at the sores and blisters that riddled our bodies, and we were gagged in order to keep from driving the nurses berserk with our screams of agony, and sometimes we were even blindfolded so that the nurses did not have to bear the torture of being watched by our agonized and pleading eyes. I spent two weeks there in a delirium, unable to do anything but feel the blisters spreading across my body.

And in my delirium, I was visited in dreams by James Shepherd, who was no longer missing an arm — the Shepherd of my youth, before he turned angry — and by Charles McLaughlin as well, who *was* angry, disappointed that I had not talked him out of his escape attempt. He was lost in the mountains, he said, and needed water again, he was dying and needed water, and then he was gone, and there was only my own fever.

We were always thirsty. In the hospital we were allowed a little coffee in the morning, and a little brandy in the evening — still blindfolded and still lashed to the hospital beds. Of the few senses still available to us, our sense of sound was the sharpest: we would hear the creak of gurney wheels each day carrying out the dead, not knowing who had survived and who had succumbed. Like divers, then, we would each descend back into the day's fevers, never knowing if each would be our own final descent as well.

Healed and back in our indoor cell, with the out-of-date *New Orleans Times-Picayune*s brought to us occasionally by Waddy Thompson, we tried to keep up with the volatile international reversals and convolutions.

Sam Houston was increasingly considering the benefits of Texas's joining the United States, but only under his republic's own terms, which would allow it to secede any time it wished. He knew that Texas would be a more attractive annexation package if he could effect an armistice with Texas's most troublesome neighbor, Mexico. Santa Anna, renegade warrior and tyrant, was also interested in an armistice, though for different reasons: his army had run out of food and supplies and needed to take a breather if they were to keep alive at all the dream of recapturing Texas.

Sam Houston, the most manipulative politician the young republic had produced to date, let Britain work toward the brokering of that armistice while he continued to pretend to be interested in the cowardly Robinson plan, hatched from one of our own prisoners in the Castle of Perve, in which Texas would actually rejoin Mexico, though with some autonomy retained. Nothing could have pleased Great Britain more, neither Santa Anna; and nothing could have made the United States more anxious, and in turn more eager to annex Texas. And in the weeks and months following our slow recovery from the typhus, we wondered if the proposed armistice might lead to our ultimate release.

*   *   *

Sam Houston continued to manipulate the British, Santa Anna, and the United States masterfully, and it occurred to us daily that if he was successful in the armistice, then Mexico might release us as a symbol of the newfound goodwill and cease-fire between the two countries.

Back in Texas, the newly elected House member Thomas Jefferson Green, not understanding that Houston's discussions with Robinson and Santa Anna were but a feint, was haranguing Houston like a bulldog, as were some of our other successful escapees, who would not forget those whom they had been forced to leave behind. We read with gusto of how they kept up the drumbeat for our release, forcing it to become an issue for Sam Houston, so that gradually that demand became part and parcel of the armistice talks.

A newspaperman named Francis Moore was particularly incensed by the Robinson plan and railed that the blood of the patriots at the Alamo and San Jacinto, in addition to the "heroism" of the Mier Expedition, would be in vain were Texas to be annexed by either Mexico or the United States; and many of the letters now making their way out of the Castle of Perve contained the same complaints.

"We hear that annexation of Texas to the United States will take place," wrote nineteen-year-old Joseph McCutchan from our dark, damp dungeon. "If I could for myself exercise influence it would be to say to Texas and the Texians hold dear those rights so dearly bought and promptly payed for in the blood and misery of your countrymen. Part not so freely with that which has cost you your best citizens at the Alamo, Goliad, and San Jacinto. Remain a nation yourselves, or Nobly Perish!"

And in a letter to the *Telegraph* and *Texas Register*, Mc-Cutchan wrote, "We are not much elated with the idea of Texas sallying under another nation for protection . . . as for myself (and it is, I believe, the opinion of the majority) — let me die — let me perish, neglected, and obscure in prison — let my frame sink under cruelties such as man never endured — let me go among the unnumbered (and innumerable) dead — and, in short, let my body decay in obscurity and my name sink into oblivion! But annex not Texas to *any* government."

A tentative, informal armistice was finally agreed on between Houston and Santa Anna as a preliminary step toward annexation, but loose gangs of Texas irregulars began scourging the Rio Grande again — without Houston's encouragement or permission, this time — harassing and sometimes murdering Mexican citizens living on both sides of the tenuous border, particularly in a remote region known as the Nueces Strip.

Houston was forced to put the entire area under martial law, authorizing Captain Jack Hays and the Texas Rangers to restore peace, which they were eventually able to do, though not before one especially notorious band of renegades known as the Man-Slayers had killed dozens of Mexican nationals on both sides of the river, forcing Santa Anna to call an end to the brief armistice. He had not yet saved enough money to go back to war, and he no longer had British support for war as he had in the past, but Santa Anna had to pretend that he was ready and willing to fight. Our chances, which had seemed brighter during the armistice, were now dashed by bandits whose actions were little different from our own.

Still weakened by typhus, we resumed digging late at night, clawing at the stony earth with our bare hands. Our knuckles were bloodied, our fingertips raw, but the guards didn't seem to notice, and as we dug deeper, the sound of the river became louder and clearer: it sounded as if it were running faster.

Waddy Thompson had fallen in love with a young Mexican woman, a general's daughter, in Mexico City. At the age of sixty-eight, he was about to retire, and he planned to remain in Mexico.

He came to visit us: an old man made young again, even if only for a while longer. He had bittersweet news; his labors had borne fruit, although unfortunately not for us.

Held elsewhere in the castle was another regiment of Texas prisoners who had been taken hostage during one of General Woll's last invasions into Texas. Santa Anna wished to reward Waddy Thompson for his service as ambassador by releasing some of Woll's captives and asked Thompson to submit a list of prisoners who should receive highest priority.

Thompson asked that we be considered for release along with Woll's prisoners, but Santa Anna held firm, reiterating his position — and it was an accurate one — that we were thieves, murderers, and pillagers, not soldiers. He would consider only some of Woll's captives, and asked again for a list of "the important ones."

"How can I distinguish between men," Thompson responded, "all strangers to me personally, whose cases are in all respects identical, and why should you?"

Santa Anna ended up signing an executive proclamation that released all of Woll's prisoners. Thompson reported to his superiors in the United States, "Nothing could have been more handsome than the manner in which this release was executed, and I am sure I have never experienced a more heartfelt pleasure."

He sat quietly among us. Our number was down to seventy-three by that point, so he was able to address all of us at once.

"I have failed at this aspect of my job," he said, speaking quietly. He looked around at each of us, his eyes as haunted and sorrowful as if it were his actions and not our own that had sealed our doom. His eyes settled on our torn and scabrous hands — he knew nothing of our second tunnel — and then told us that although it would be inappropriate for him to counsel escape, and that we would surely be executed if captured, the time might be drawing nigh for that last resort.

"I am about to marry a beautiful, loving woman," he said. He gestured at our dark cell. "I am about to leave all of this behind." He shook his head. "My failure to get you released has been the greatest regret of my professional life."

We were to see Thompson only once again. A week later — following a feast in his honor — General Woll's captives were escorted from the castle, marching in single file across the drawbridge, into the noonday sun. We were all gathered in the courtyard to watch their march to freedom, and a few of the more daring from our expedition, Bigfoot Wallace among them, had maneuvered themselves into position to slip into the ranks of Woll's captives to march out with them: and they did so, passing successfully out of the fort and all the way across the drawbridge. They made it a hundred yards out into the desert before one of the guards recognized them, ordered them out of the line, and returned them to the castle.

But rather than being executed, as was customary protocol for anyone caught attempting an escape, the returning prisoners were treated with good-natured ridicule and hoots of derision from the soldiers. And, as if in reward for the entertainment provided, we received extra rations that night, but after eating we did not play cards or sing or dance but sat around in morose silence, the castle feeling emptier and lonelier than it had before.

We waited for midnight, and then beyond, so that we could begin quietly digging.

The new U.S. ambassador to Mexico, Wilson Shannon, met with us, and we could see right away that he was not proud of his post, that he found the entire country disagreeable and resented in particular that part of his duty that called him to the Castle of Perve. He spoke no Spanish (neither would he trouble himself to learn any), and he was aghast at our stumbling, mumbling, nearly naked condition, and by the autumn swelter, and by the lice. He had had to ride a mule to Perote, accompanied by an armed regiment to protect him against bandits, and the day he arrived the entire country had been resounding with the steady fire of cannons, rifles, and pistols. At first we had believed the country to be under attack, but we soon learned that the shots were being fired in mourning for the death of Santa Anna's wife, Doña Inés, who, though only thirty-three, had died that day after a long illness.

We were astounded by how little Shannon knew about our circumstances, or about Texas, or Mexico. It seemed that Fisher and Wallace and myself spent far more time filling him in on key details than he did in giving us any information.

We showed Shannon our tunnel, which was nearly completed. We posted a sentry by our door to warn us if one of the Mexican guards approached, and lifted the tiles and offered to take him down into the tunnel, toward the sound of that river that none of us had ever seen.

Shannon recoiled in horror and bid us to replace the tiles quickly. He urged us not to attempt escape — indeed, to fill the tunnel back in — though he had no plans for getting us released. We reminded him that with the collapse of the Texas-Mexico armistice and then the failure of the United States to annex Texas there was no longer any hope of Santa Anna releasing us.

Shannon stared at us blankly, then rose to leave. It was evening, and the sound of cannons and muskets filled the night, as they had all during the day. Bigfoot Wallace, his legs bowed and scarred by many months in chains, rose also, and placed his big hand on Shannon's shoulder. "How about if you stay in here and try and think things through and I'll walk out and tell them we decided to trade places for a while? And how about if I just give you a swift boot in the ass right now, to hurry things along?"

Shannon blanched, slipped free of the grasp of that huge hand, and rapped on the door for the sentries to let him out.

After Shannon was gone we settled in for our regular evening activities, even as outside the night continued to fracture with the concussive sounds of mourning and ceremony: and we waited for later in the night, when we could resume digging.

Weeks later, war resumed between Mexico and Texas, but Waddy Thompson, even in retirement, continued to work on our behalf. One morning, less than a week after the burial of Doña Inés, Thompson reappeared in our dungeon (we had decided to push through to the river that very night; we had finished drilling our bunks with dowels and pegs so that they could be disassembled, taken down into the tunnel, then reassembled into rafts, below ground) and told us to take heart, that our old nemesis, General Ampudia, who had been responsible for our initial capture so long ago in Ciudad Mier, had gotten involved in an international incident down near the Yucatán, which might have some bearing on attempts to release us.

Ampudia had captured a band of insurgents — some native, others foreign mercenaries — and although the captured band had raised a white flag of surrender, Ampudia had executed them all, and, like his associate Canales some years earlier, had decapitated the rebel leader, fried his head in oil, and displayed it in an iron cage for several days.

Among the victims had been three Americans, in addition to several French, British, and Spanish citizens.

Thompson said, "Shannon is meeting with Santa Anna at this very moment. The world is crumbling around Santa Anna. You have outlasted him. Take heart." He placed his hand on Fisher's shoulder. "Hold on to your men for one more day," he said. "You have served and led and advised them honorably. Hold on for one more day."

We had all already made the commitment to escape that night. Even I had decided to go after all my earlier years of indecision. We had all decided to go, strong or weak, lame or infirm, no matter: all of us, with Fisher following at the rear. There was a light rain falling that day; the conditions could not have been better.

"All right," Fisher said slowly, quietly, speaking to Thompson. "I will trust you."

We sat up all through the night, waiting. The tunnel was finished — we had lowered our lit candles into it, had seen the dark river below. We were ready to go, but we sat, and we waited.

In the morning, when the guards usually came with our breakfast, instead an armed regiment arrived in dress uniforms, and our hearts fell, believing that we were about to be executed. Someone, we feared — Shannon, perhaps — had informed them of the tunnel.

We were escorted into a large empty room, in which there was but a single long desk, with one man, a general, seated in a chair behind it.

Two candles were burning in the room, one on either side of a big Bible that sat on the desk. Next to the Bible was a ledger; one by one we were asked, or commanded, to step forward and sign the ledger and, in exchange for our freedom, swear never to take up arms against Mexico again.

Scarcely believing what was happening, and moving as if in a dream, we filed to the desk and signed our name or mark, laid our palsied hands on the Bible, and swore allegiance to this pact, and then were escorted into the courtyard.

Weeping, cheering, limping, embracing one another and even our former captors, we trembled as the chains were peeled from our scarred and rotting ankles. We were still weeping as Fisher ordered us into formation.

The day was bright and clear and cool, the sky washed blue from the previous day's rain, and we could smell the fragrance of the desert in bloom. Fisher commanded us to march, and in formation we filed across the drawbridge, past the white swans and onto the road that led to Vera Cruz, while the guards at the Castle of Perve shouted their good wishes and fired their cannons to cheer our great fortune. Thompson and Shannon had arranged for a steamer to be waiting for us in Vera Cruz, and within two weeks we would be back home.

Perhaps I should not have followed the other seventy-two men to Vera Cruz, as I should not have followed them into Mexico. Maybe my true path, the one laid down for me even before my birth — as might all men, of all nations, have various paths laid down before them, to choose, or not to choose — lay in the direction of Mexico City, and a return to Clara. As a released man, finally, if not yet free, I might have been able to impress myself upon Bustamente and claim and make a life with Clara, in either her country or mine, no matter.

I hesitated after crossing the bridge. I was still a young man, barely seventeen. I had time to burn, a whole life to burn. Below me, the swans were paddling in elegant patterns that seemed somehow linked and connected to every-thing else in the world.

My fellow soldiers were wasting no time. They were marching on, shouting and crying in disbelief at their good fortune.

I hurried on to catch them.

EPILOGUE

I HAVE SPENT the fifty years since in the rolling hills near Navasota, growing pecans and corn and cotton and peaches. I survived the ensuing U.S. war with Mexico, following Texas's annexation by the United States, and the Indian wars, which are only now ending, and the Civil War, or War for Southern Independence Against the Northern Aggression, as many in this state called it, though I was not one of them. I have seen a tenuous, uncertain nation bloom into a confident state: too confident at times, it seems to me, in the attitude that because its freedom was born of blood rather than diplomacy, that is the only true and right way.

Even now, however, I think that if anyone were to attempt to take or ruin this land, I would cross over that river yet again; that even knowing what I know, and having seen what I have seen, I might yet still be pulled across — an old man, now — as incapable of change in that regard as the turn of the seasons and the secrets of the soil itself.

Seventy-three of us came home from the Castle of Perve.

Some men came home to nothing; it was as if their lives had ceased from the moment that they had first crossed the border. Willis Coplan, for example, came home to a gravestone in his front yard that already bore his name, and with his wife remarried and living there with her new husband and family.

For a while Charles McLaughlin worked as an illustrator for some of the newspapers that had agitated for our release, and then, following Texas's annexation to the United States, he went to Paris, not as an act of political dissent but merely to pursue his education. For years I received hand-drawn Christmas cards from him as he traveled farther east — to China, and India, and Borneo — before I finally stopped hearing from him around the age of thirty.

Other men, alas, were corrupted into the habit of war, beyond any hope of reclamation. Even in peace, they found more war. Colonel Fisher, Bigfoot Wallace, Samuel Walker, and others rode with the Texas Rangers, even after the annexation, fighting Comanches as well as Mexicans, and soon earned a name for their cruelty and tortures. Walker, who had buried a dime in the soil at Perote, vowing to come back and reclaim it some day with the interest of vengeance, did just that, leading a regiment back into Perote during the U.S.-Mexican War of 1846. He was shot dead while leading that charge but succeeded in routing the town and freeing all the prisoners — the scalawags, vermin, and unjustly imprisoned alike — and as he lay dying, his men fell prostrate across his chest, weeping for the loss of their captain.

It was the same as it had always been. Those who did not die in battle were cursed to grow old and rheumy, forgotten and untended, such as Bigfoot Wallace himself, retired out on a hardscrabble ranch west of San Antonio, far too old for war, finally, but knowing nothing else. Having killed a thousand men perhaps, by bullet, knife, and saber, and knowing nothing else; and staring, now, into the long black tunnel of the last days of his life, with no other paths, no choices or options remaining but silence and the dark vanishing.

The other night there was a warm balmy March breeze from the Gulf, and it seemed to carry every memory, every scent, from those days of hardship: memories and days and months and then years that I have labored to forget, as if working them to compost, cloaking them in the viny growth of pumpkins and squash, and in the military precision of countless rows of corn, and in the leafy green breath of peas and beans.

The breeze blew open my doors and windows, banged open a cabinet, and knocked an empty tin cup from the counter, awakening me; and when I arose, it seemed then that all those memories had not been riven to soil and worm food but had been stored away somewhere, ever bright and unharmed — in my cabinets, perhaps — and ready to return. It seemed that they *were* returning, spilling and sliding from the empty shelves, or that they were the breeze itself: and I was frightened, as I should have been but was not, the first time, when Green and Fisher came riding into town so long ago, and I was overwhelmed too with sadness, and I found myself weeping.

I walked outside, my face damp, frightened and lonely: as if all I had strived for in fifty years, all I had labored to bury and convert to good, had been for naught, had returned with but a single whim of the wind.

The fields were ready for planting, had been plowed but not yet seeded. I had been drawing maps, making plans for what crop would go where, and in what quantity. How they would interact with one another in their various placements and positions, how one would rise while another would fall. Which ones would serve and give to the soil, and which ones would take from and deplete — for a little while — that same soil.

The rows of furrows stretched comfortingly before me in the silver moonlight: a crescent moon was setting behind the bare pecan trees at the far edge of the field, down by the river. The rows were perfect, evenly spaced, and yet appeared to be converging across the field's great distance to but a single point, down by those trees.

My eyes adjusted to the moon's light, and I saw then that all was not perfect, that something had marred the furrows. Something had passed transversely across them, crumbling their ridges and compacting the previously loosened and sifted soil.

The marring was far too large to be the stippled tiny hoofs of deer, and yet too even for the stumbling destruction of cattle or horse. There was instead a wild elegance to the script, and an ominousness.

I walked out into the field toward those tracks, being careful not to disrupt any of the ridges I had so carefully plowed. When I came to the tracks — so fresh that I knew they had been made only moments earlier — I crouched and examined them, and I recognized them to be those of a great cat, a jaguar, its prints wider than the spread of my hand: tracks such as I had seen in my travels of half a century ago, and even occasionally in the country around my home as a child, before settlers and civilization killed all the jaguars off.

Something moved at the far end of the field, back in the trees' darkness; something dark stirred within the darkness, then was gone.

I was barefooted, but the night was warm and I felt no chill. I set out across the field in the moonlight, following the script of those fresh tracks down toward the trees.

ACKNOWLEDGMENTS

In the fall of 1842, with the new Republic of Texas barely six years old, and tensions between Mexico and Texas still raw and rife — as they would continue to be, even after Texas was ultimately admitted to the United States — a small army of Texas volunteers invaded Mexico in defiance of the Texas president Sam Houston's explicit orders, though perhaps with his contradictory, tacit assent, off the record. This much seems true: one leader, William S. Fisher, defied the expedition's leader, Alexander Somervell, and crossed over the Texas-Mexico border, seeking war.

The militia volunteers committed atrocities on both sides of the border (as many of them had already committed against the Comanches, in the years preceding their adventure in Old Mexico). Decapitations, inhumane treatment of prisoners, questionable documents, economic inabilities to wage sustained war, political ambitions: all that exists now existed then. For readers interested in the facts of this period, works by the great Texas historian T. R. Fehrenbach, such as *Lone Star*, would be a fine beginning point, as would the invaluable *Soldiers of Misfortune:*

The Somervell and Mier Expeditions by Sam W. Haynes, and *Mier Expedition Diary: A Texas Prisoner's Account*, by Joseph D. McCutchan, edited by Joseph Milton Nance. *The Adventures of Bigfoot Wallace* by John Duval, circa 1870, is an interesting read, as is Fanny Gooch Inglehart's 1910 chronicle *The Boy Captive of the Texas Mier Expedition: A Thrilling Episode of the Texas Republic.*

It's standard practice for novelists trafficking in history to establish the traditional caveat along the lines of "Any inaccuracies are solely the responsibility of the author, not the subjects," etc.; but in this instance, the novelist has traveled some distance beyond what might be termed "historical fiction."

Certain things are factual, others imagined: all, one hopes, are true to the spirit of this novel, if nothing else. General Somervell, a significant part of the historical raid, is largely absent in this accounting, which focuses, through a fictional narrator, on the leadership of two other Texans, Thomas Jefferson Green and William Fisher. This book is not intended to be read as a replacement for or even a supplement to Texas history, but instead has arisen from that history and heritage. The novel was written in the first days of the invasion of Baghdad; for that emotional truth I can claim no evasion or caveat. Certain historical timelines and key incidents are factual. For others I found no reference beyond the truth of my own engagement with this story, its landscape, and the nature of men and nations at war.

I'm grateful, as ever, to my editors — Harry Foster and Alison Kerr Miller — and for help by Beth Kluckhohn and Will Vincent, and my typist, Angi Young, and to Robert Overholtzer and Rodrigo Corral. I'm grateful also for the editing of Tom Jenks and Carol Edgarian of *Narrative* magazine, which serialized this novel — and to my agent, Bob Dattila, and to Terry Jones for help with Spanish translations, and the biologist Jerry Scoville for help with the natural history of Mexico.

The Book of Yaak

Bass delves into the soul of one of the last great wild places in the United States, the Yaak Valley of northwestern Montana.

ISBN-13: 978-0-395-87746-3
ISBN-10: 0-395-87746-6

Colter: The True Story of the Best Dog I Ever Had

Bass captures the essence of canine companionship with this vivid account of his relationship with Colter, a German shorthair pup.

ISBN-13: 978-0-618-12736-8
ISBN-10: 0-618-12736-4

The Diezmo: A Novel

At once a gut-wrenching parable of war and a stirring coming-of-age adventure, this is a novel about the Mier Expedition, one of the most absurd and tragic military adventures in American history.

ISBN-13: 978-0-618-71050-8
ISBN-10: 0-618-71050-7

The Hermit's Story: Stories

Selected as a Los Angeles Times Book of the Year, this collection of ten remarkable stories explores the near-mythical connections between man and nature.

ISBN-13: 978-0-618-38044-2
ISBN-10: 0-618-38044-2

In the Loyal Mountains: Stories

Each of these ten dazzling short stories embraces vibrant images of ordinary life and exuberant descriptions of nature.

ISBN-13: 978-0-395-87747-0
ISBN-10: 0-395-87747-4

The Lost Grizzlies: A Search for Survivors in the Wilderness of Colorado

Bass describes the courage, hope, and friendships at the heart of the search for grizzlies in the San Juan Mountains.

ISBN-13: 978-0-395-85700-7
ISBN-10: 0-395-85700-7

The Ninemile Wolves

Following the fate of a modern wolf pack, Bass charts the deeply conflicted relationship between man and beast.

ISBN-13: 978-0-618-26302-8
ISBN-10: 0-618-26302-0

The Sky, the Stars, the Wilderness: Novellas

Magical, passionate, and lyrical, this collection of three novellas received the Mountains and Plains Booksellers Award for Fiction.

ISBN-13: 978-0-395-92475-4
ISBN-10: 0-395-92475-8

Where the Sea Used to Be: A Novel

Bass's first full-length novel is the story of a struggle between a father and his daughter for the souls of two men — his protégés, her lovers.

ISBN-13: 978-0-395-95781-3
ISBN-10: 0-395-95781-8

Winter: Notes from Montana

In a celebration of winter in a remote, sparsely populated valley of Montana, Bass describes the slow-motion quality of life and the dangers of the wilderness.

ISBN-13: 978-0-395-61150-0
ISBN-10: 0-395-61150-4